A Candlelight Ecstasy Romance®

"YOU COULD USE SOME SWEETENING UP," MEG INFORMED HIM.

"What would you suggest?" Jonathan asked.

"I don't know. A cold glass of cider?"

"You're an optimist, Margaret T. I need a lot more than a glass of cider."

She wanted to ask why, but she knew it was time to change the subject. "Art said you wanted me."

Jonathan grinned. "Now you're talking, Margaret T. Just how sweet are you?"

"I'm not known for being sweet at all."

"Ah," he said, his grin fading to a delicious smile. "A tart?"

"Adjective, not noun. If we were comparing me to an apple . . ."

"You'd be ripe for the picking?" Jonathan asked with a twinkle in his eye.

CANDLELIGHT ECSTASY ROMANCES®

APPLE OF MY EYE

Carla Neggers

A CANDLELIGHT ECSTASY ROMANCE®

Published by
Dell Publishing Co., Inc.
1 Dag Hammarskjold Plaza
New York, New York 10017

Dell ® TM 681510, Dell Publishing Co., Inc.

Candlelight Ecstasy Romance®, 1,203,540, is a registered
trademark of Dell Publishing Co., Inc., New York, New York.

ISBN: 0-440-10283-9

Printed in the United States of America

First printing—February 1985

To Denise

To Our Readers:

We have been delighted with your enthusiastic response to Candlelight Ecstasy Romances®, and we thank you for the interest you have shown in this exciting series.

In the upcoming months we will continue to present the distinctive, sensuous love stories you have come to expect only from Ecstasy. We look forward to bringing you many more books from your favorite authors and also the very finest work from new authors of contemporary romantic fiction.

As always, we are striving to present the unique, absorbing love stories that you enjoy most—books that are more than ordinary romance.

Your suggestions and comments are always welcome. Please write to us at the address below.

Sincerely,

The Editors
Candlelight Romances
1 Dag Hammarskjold Plaza
New York, New York 10017

CHAPTER ONE

"Name?"

"Oakes," Meg replied automatically, having decided three apple orchards ago not to give a false name. Being furtive was enough of a chore without having to remember some silly alias. If she ever did find herself face-to-face with Ross Greening, he wouldn't know who Meg Oakes was anyway. *Keep it simple,* she had told herself.

"Meg Oakes," she went on.

She watched the man who was supposedly interviewing her jot down the information. He hadn't given her even a perfunctory glance since she'd walked into the rustic office ten seconds ago. Now Meg began to wonder what lay beneath that mop of auburn-tinted dark hair. When people interviewed her, she generally liked to know what they looked like. Sometimes *not* knowing would have brightened her day, but nevertheless it was just one of those things. She didn't think she'd ever been interviewed by a mop of hair.

Realizing she could stare all she wanted to—he'd never notice—Meg duly noted his broad, tanned hand. He also had broad shoulders, probably tanned, and she duly noted them too.

Then she said unnecessarily, "Margaret, not Megan." She paused so he could respond, but he didn't. So she added, "Margaret T."

She heard the subtle note of sarcasm in her voice, but the man behind the cluttered oak desk either hadn't or chose to ignore it. Generally her sarcasm wasn't subtle, and rarely did anyone ignore it. But this wasn't New York, Meg reminded herself; maybe the standards for sarcasm were different.

"Address?" he asked.

So far she liked his deep baritone voice, but, then, he'd only spoken two words. Still, it and the shoulders and the big hands indicated strength and a certain burliness. And the flannel shirt. It was red plaid and, of course, well worn. Meg smiled to herself: Would this man drink Perrier? Ha! She wondered what he would do if she clicked her heels together and saluted. Ordinarily, of course, she wouldn't have hesitated to find out, but she had promised Wolfe she'd behave. Wolfe had called her a "sarcastic little chit" more than once during her eight weeks as his newest associate. She had argued she was simply blunt and sometimes injudiciously honest, but he nonetheless made her promise to keep a bridle on her tongue during her search for Ross Greening.

Her *reluctant* search for Ross Greening. As far as she was concerned, authors who didn't want to be found by their former agents shouldn't be found by their former agents.

Wolfe, naturally, didn't agree.

She remembered she was supposed to be giving her address and said, somewhat abruptly, "South Main, Rocky Springs." McGavock Orchards was in New

Rocky Springs. There was also, she had learned, an East Rocky Springs and a South Rocky Springs in this particular corner of Connecticut. "Has a nice ring to it, doesn't it?"

He grunted and wrote.

"I live above the town library."

Suddenly he whirled around on the ancient secretarial chair. Meg thought she'd done something desperately wrong, but he merely stuck his pencil in a pencil sharpener and started cranking. She caught a glimpse of a strong, clean shaven jaw. A beard would have been more fitting on this burly man, she thought.

"Sounds romantic, doesn't it?" she said, idly trying to picture him in a tuxedo. What he had on complemented his muscular physique, but, Meg realized, so would just about anything close to the right size. "It's pretty quiet except for story hour. Three- and four-year-olds can get amazingly loud. The Berenstain Bears seem to be the current favorites."

He whirled back around to the desk just as quickly as he had whirled to the pencil sharpener, and before Meg could decide whether the strong jaw went with an equally strong face, he had resumed his position. He'd sharpened the pencil practically down to its eraser. It looked silly in his big hand. No doubt he was more accustomed to wielding a chain saw than a stubby pencil.

Chain saws—what was it about chain saws? *Ross Greening!* Supposedly he had an eighty-stitch scar on one of his thighs. This single-minded individual before her now looked as if he could have had more than one run-in with a chain saw, but that wouldn't necessarily mean he was Ross Greening. Just careless with chain

13

saws. Wolfe had been unable to render an adequate description of Ross Greening—brown hair, over six feet—but he *had* mentioned the missing author's scar, the result of a chain saw mishap several years ago. Meg had squirmed at the thought of turning a chain saw loose on a human thigh, but Wolfe was unsympathetic: "The damned fool had to cancel a promotion tour for his book."

Meg, however, realized she couldn't very well tell any of her suspects to stand up and drop his drawers. Certainly not this one. Besides, he wasn't Ross Greening. Ross Greening wanted to *avoid* people. He would have had the teenagers—and one adult—applying for temporary jobs picking apples fill out the applications themselves, as had the other three orchards Meg had been to. Obviously the man interviewing her wasn't enjoying himself, and a reclusive writer with millions of books sold would have been able to extricate himself from a task he didn't enjoy.

"Social security number?"

Apparently he wasn't impressed with her apartment above the Rocky Springs Free Town Library, she thought, and rattled off the obligatory nine numerals. Maybe Ross Greening wasn't even in Connecticut. Maybe Wolfe was off his rocker, and Greening was in Nova Scotia. Or Tucson. Or Kenya. Why Rocky Springs, Connecticut, for heaven's sake? Meg had suggested that Greening just might be dead, but Wolfe had dismissed the possibility. "He wouldn't dare die before I catch up with him," the high-powered literary agent had declared.

"Well?"

Meg jumped and realized she had missed his next

question. "I'm sorry," she said, not meaning it. "I didn't hear you. The smell of apples—"

"Shouldn't affect your hearing," he finished, looking up at her for the first time. "Well, I see you are."

Meg tried to reconcile the face with the voice, the hands, and the broad shoulders. She had expected a brawny face, weather-beaten, not too bright. *Burly.* Instead she detected intelligence and refinement in the quick gray-green eyes, the straight nose, the sculpted mouth, the strong jaw.

Ross Greening?

No, impossible. Still, Wolfe had said his missing author had brown hair and an impressive physique. The man sitting on the other side of the oak desk had both. Meg wondered if she should call Wolfe that evening and ask him if Greening also had gray-green eyes. She had asked about eyes that crazy day in New York two weeks ago, but Wolfe's only comment had been, "He has two."

She checked her rampant thoughts and asked, "You can see I'm what?"

"Sixteen."

At that moment she noticed an impertinence in those same gray-green eyes. They were her only hint that he was amused, even curious. He was also staring at her. She had seen enough of her apple picking competition to know she was different, and not just older. The teenagers had all worn denim and sneakers or decrepit hiking boots. Meg wore freshly dry-cleaned teal blue corduroy slacks, a Viyella shirt with a burgundy ribbon tied at the neckline, and casual Pappagallo shoes with a one-inch heel. At the last minute she had decided to forego a full face of cosmetics and just slapped on a little tinted lip gloss. She had thought she looked smartly casual.

"Oh, at least," she said, smiling.

He didn't smile back, but neither did he look as surly as she had expected. "I'll need your birthdate," he said.

"Why?"

"Ask the government."

"Oh."

Meg had never before lied about her age, but now she was tempted. Applying for apple picking jobs had started out as a ruse so she could legitimately worm her way into orchards and perhaps find Ross Greening. Now it didn't matter to her if Greening grew apples or prunes or nothing at all. She wanted the job. She wanted to get out among the apple trees and work and sweat in the crisp autumn air. She wanted to pick apples, dammit!

But she doubted that the people who ran McGavock Orchards would be any more enlightened than those at the three other orchards in the area, who had obviously thought a thirty-year-old woman should be doing almost anything but picking apples. Eighteen? She hadn't looked eighteen even when she *was* eighteen. Twenty-one? He'd never believe it. *Okay,* she thought, *I'll split the difference and call it twenty-five.* She did some quick subtraction in her head and gave him the fictitious date.

She learned just how quick and intelligent those gray-green eyes were when they flashed up at her. He put down his two-inch pencil and stuck out a callused hand. "Your driver's license, please."

"My—Why?"

16

"Isn't it passé for a woman to lie about her age?"

"Isn't it *rude* for a man not to believe a woman who lies about her age?"

"Then you are lying."

"My birthday *is* July 24."

"Ten years earlier than what you said."

"Ten!"

"Fifteen?"

"Cad."

He grinned, the corners of his eyes crinkling and a dimple appearing in each cheek. Meg didn't relax, but she did feel better. That he was Ross Greening was now completely and totally impossible. Wolfe would have *had* to mention those dimples. The manager of McGavock Orchards was showing yet another side of himself, this one, she thought, altogether adorable. The effect was incredible: He was at once infuriating, endearing, and seductive. He tapped the point of his pencil on the index card and said, holding back another grin, "That's what goes down here if you don't cough up the truth, Ms. Oakes."

"Add five years."

"To which?"

"The twenty-five!"

She gave him credit for not looking too victorious as he printed the correct date. "And I'll need a phone number," he said, businesslike.

"I don't have a phone."

"So you're new in town. I thought so." He dropped the card into a shoebox and nodded at her. "Okay, Ms. Oakes, I'll be in touch."

Meg had been around enough personnel offices to

know when she'd been tossed into the reject pile. "That, sir," she said disdainfully, "is a platitude."

Not giving him a chance to respond, she pivoted on her toes and walked out. He didn't say a word, but somehow she didn't think it was because she'd left him speechless. She stormed out of the office into the retail area of the converted barn and moaned at the spicy, enticing scent of freshly baked apple dumplings. Curse the man! She'd planned to buy a dumpling and sit outside at a picnic table with it and a cup of coffee, but now on principle she couldn't. She reared back her shoulders and bravely walked through the snack area, past the benches of apples and cider, and , . . *bread!* Oh, God, she thought, homemade oatmeal bread! Surreptitiously she stuck out a hand and touched the top of a wrapped loaf.

It was still warm.

Cursing Michael Wolfe for ever getting her into this situation, Meg made her way outside. The sun was warm, the sky blue and cloudless, the air clear and crisp. A perfect late September afternoon in southern New England. Meg glanced at the teenagers eating apples and dumplings on the picnic tables on a grassy slope overlooking the orchards.

Children!

She flounced over to her car—a Honda, the only new vehicle in the unpaved parking area—and couldn't help glancing at herself in the rearview mirror. No wrinkles, no gray hair, no little stamp on her forehead that said "Over the hill." Just smooth ivory skin, golden eyes, and short, wavy golden hair.

God, she thought, *I've never felt so old!*

So she cursed the manager of McGavock Orchards

for making her feel like Grandma Moses, and while she was at it she cursed Ross Greening as well. If he'd just kept in touch with his erstwhile agent, she wouldn't be in this miserable corner of Connecticut.

She started up the car and tried to tell herself she was being unfair. She *was* thirty, after all, and she supposed she looked it. Not for any tangible reasons, she knew, but she herself could see the invisible scars that told people that she was a woman, not a girl, that she was no longer eighteen or even twenty-five.

But in *her* world thirty was young, experienced, desirable, knowledgeable. It sure as hell wasn't old, and it certainly didn't mean she wasn't capable of picking a few crummy apples!

Meg's irritation festered during the ride along winding country roads back into town. Even the cheerful hello from the librarian and the welcome coziness of her little apartment didn't soothe her. She was just plain mad. And she had three good reasons for her lousy mood: her employer, her wouldn't-be employer, and her—What *was* Ross Greening? She dumped out the last of a leftover glass of iced tea and thought a moment. Greening was nothing to her. She liked his books, but she'd never even met the man, didn't know much about him, and yet . . .

"And yet I'm after him," she said wearily.

Ross Greening was her quarry.

She set the glass down hard on the countertop—red Formica—and tried to think about what she would do with the three sparsely furnished rooms if she actually planned on living there.

Living in Rocky Springs? She shuddered at the

thought. What on earth would she do with herself? She'd rather think about Greening and Wolfe and the man with the gray-green eyes who thought thirty was over the hill.

"A bounty hunter," she muttered disgustedly. "I feel like a bounty hunter!"

She envisioned herself hog-tying Greening and hauling him off to New York on her white steed.

And then somehow Greening, whom she'd never met, became the dark-haired man in the red-plaid flannel shirt, whom she'd met and hoped never to see again.

She doubted he'd stand for any hog-tying.

"Why do you keep thinking about him?"

Nerves, she thought, making herself a fresh glass of iced tea. She'd been looking for Ross Greening for three days and had come up with nothing more substantial than what she had when she left New York. Which wasn't much, thanks to Wolfe.

As she tried to stir the lumps of instant tea, Meg for the very first time found herself actually hoping she'd catch up with Ross Greening. It was *his* fault she'd opened herself up to such abuse from four Connecticut apple orchards. If the foolish man hadn't tried to give Michael Wolfe the slip, she would be back in Manhattan critiquing manuscripts like she was supposed to instead of getting so aggravated over a ridiculous apple picking job.

She would call Wolfe and give him a huge chunk of her mind. Then she'd feel better. But how? She didn't have a telephone. And she wasn't about to rail at a powerful New York literary agent on the pay phone next to the meat counter at Granger's Market.

So she took her glass of lumpy iced tea out to the living room, where she'd set up her venerable old typewriter on the sturdy desk that had come with the apartment. Wolfe didn't know she'd packed her typewriter, and he wouldn't have approved if he did know. "Go incognito, Oakes," he had decreed. "Pretend you're a housewife from the suburbs who's decided to go out and find herself or something dumb like that. Got a pair of espadrilles?" Meg had suggested she go as a single woman, which she was, who had decided to find some peace and quiet to finish her dissertation. Wolfe had vetoed the idea: "Naw, you don't look like an egghead." Meg pointed out that she didn't look like a suburban housewife either, but Wolfe had insisted espadrilles would do the trick.

She'd ended up ignoring all his decrees and doing it her way, which amounted to playing it by ear. No one had asked her why she'd come to Rocky Springs, so she hadn't had to come up with an explanation. And how damning could a typewriter be?

She took a swallow of tea, tried not to grimace, and rolled in a sheet of her personal stationery. She'd write to Wolfe. She'd let him know just how much trouble his asinine assignment was causing his newest associate.

Ooh, she thought, rubbing her fingertips together, *this is going to feel so good!*

She typed the date and then stopped.

"Margaret," she said aloud, "do you remember why you had a thousand sheets of this lovely ebony-on-ecru stationery printed in the first place?"

She remembered: For months she had had no professional stationery to use. And she had no professional stationery because she had no job. And she had no job because she'd been fired. Outplaced, as it were.

Perhaps, she thought, a snippy note to the man who'd plucked her out of unemployment lines, who'd rescued her from cashing in her last money market certificate, who'd taken a chance on her—perhaps it just wasn't a good idea.

After all, hadn't Wolfe shown great faith in her when he sent her after his top writer? Never mind that the task was of dubious ethics. *That,* she thought, wasn't the point. The point was that eight weeks ago she had been flattered and relieved and *thrilled* to be on Wolfe's payroll, and it would be stupid to jeopardize her job now because some jerk thought she was too old to pick apples—

"That's it!"

The manager of McGavock Orchards was the one who'd lit her fuse, so why not write to *his* boss? Presumably he was a McGavock, and to have hired a manager like that, he must undoubtedly be male. She'd vent her spleen on *him.* The words came in a flurry of indignation:

Dear Mr. McGavock:

Today I had the misfortune to apply for a temporary job picking apples at your orchards and found myself in an interview with your manager. Since he failed to introduce himself, I cannot give you his name. I would, however, urge you to discuss with him the proprieties of conducting interviews. I found him just this side of surly, and in my opinion the entire process was completely unprofessional.

Obviously I would not expect an orchard to conduct itself with the same aplomb as a large corporation, but, nonetheless, rules of good business should apply. As a public relations executive, I would like to recommend that you strive to leave a sweet taste in the mouths of those who take the time to apply to you for work—not a sour taste. Regard it as a compliment, not an imposition. You should want even those you ultimately reject to come away with a positive feeling about your company. They are, after all, potential customers.

Or, as in my case, *were.*

Sincerely,

Margaret T. Oakes

Meg proofed the letter for typographical errors, decided the tone was just as snooty and high-handed as she wanted it, and stuck it in an envelope. Ordinarily she would have waited until morning to mail the letter, but now that she lived next door to the post office, all she had to do was go downstairs, turn left, walk past Mrs. Arnold's marigolds, and there she was. So she did.

The letter was on its way to McGavock Orchards before Meg had a chance to calm down. Letter writing had always been one of her ways of easing the tensions that gnawed on her insides and gave other people in high-pressure jobs ulcers, but she rarely mailed the vituperative products of her trusty typewriter. Usually by the time she got around to buying stamps, the offending incident had been put into perspective, and she was calm and rational and onto something else. Letters to newspaper editors and presidents of large oil companies were by far her favorites. She'd written and thrown away scores of them over the years.

But Mr. McGavock would get his. Would word get around that that woman who'd moved in over the library had told off a local maverick? Ha, she hoped so! Still, it wouldn't do to become a pariah within a week of moving into town. She had a reclusive writer to find. She shrugged, decided McGavock Orchards probably had a policy of alienating people, and went off to Granger's for a quart of milk and a basket of locally grown tomatoes. She made sure they hadn't originated on McGavock property.

Two unproductive days later an envelope bearing the attractive apple logo of McGavock Orchards was in Meg's post office box. With a little cry of surprise she tore it open there in the middle of the post office and read the typed note:

Dear Ms. Oakes:

Excuse my lack of "aplomb," but why the hell would a public relations executive want to pick apples at minimum wage?

Regards,

Jonathan McGavock

His signature was just as bold as his letter. Only the curious onlooking of the postmistress and her assistant kept Meg from growling. She smiled noncommittally and stuffed the missive into her canvas bag.

When she got up to her apartment, she reread the terse little note and wondered if she should laugh or rip it to shreds.

So she decided to answer it.

Dear Mr. McGavock:

I have four years of experience picking apples in Washington state, and I presume the process— and the nonmonetary rewards—haven't changed.

Attacking my motives still doesn't excuse the surly interview to which I was subjected.

Sincerely,

Margaret Oakes

P.S. A business letter, particularly a short one, should have no more than two typographical errors, corrected or uncorrected. Yours had five. I assumed you typed it yourself. Too cheap to hire a secretary?

It wasn't until *after* Meg had posted the letter that she decided the postscript was out of order. The entire letter was probably out of order, she thought, since it was mostly lies, but she had mailed it anyway. Surely Mr. McGavock wouldn't bother to answer this time.

To distract herself, she drove out to South Rocky Springs—in the opposite direction of New Rocky Springs and McGavock Orchards—and found a pick-your-own stand. The view wasn't as magnificent as at McGavock's, and there were no apple dumplings and pies and warm oatmeal bread, but Meg picked half a bushel of Wealthies. Afterward she felt much better.

The following morning an envelope bearing the McGavock logo was in her box once again. Meg wasn't sure she liked that. How had he managed to get an answer off to her so quickly? Letter in hand, she approached the post office window. The assistant, Mrs. Hennessee, smiled. "Oh," she said, "I see you got Jonathan's letter. You *just* missed him."

"I did?"

"Yes. His box is right below yours."

"But I—he lives in the next town over, doesn't he?"

Mrs. Hennessee, a stout and efficient woman, nodded. "Yes, but there's no post office in New Rocky Springs, only rural delivery. All mail for both towns comes through here. The orchard's delivery and mailing addresses are in two different towns, and sometimes people get confused, but we usually can sort things out."

"So Mr. McGavock . . ."

"He got your letter yesterday afternoon—we put it in his box right away—and posted one to you just now."

Meg smiled thinly. She knew two facts about the renowned thriller writer she was supposed to be tracking down: One, Ross Greening wasn't his real name; two, the Michael Wolfe Literary Agency sent his royalty statements to the Rocky Springs post office. "One of the advantages of being a small town, I suppose," she mumbled.

"We know everybody."

Meg prudently resisted opening the letter until she was back upstairs above the library. Did Jonathan McGavock know he could have walked another thirty steps and saved himself twenty cents by delivering his

26

letter in person? She sighed and hoped she could avoid a face-to-face confrontation with the man.

Unless he was Ross Greening.

Or knew Ross Greening.

Absurd! She was beginning to see Ross Greenings everywhere she went! Behind every juniper bush and in every apple tree. Maybe he didn't exist. Maybe he was a she, and the man Wolfe had described was just some male model hired by the *real* Ross Greening. During the past week Meg had considered every possibility.

As she tore open the envelope she took note of the post office box number—Mrs. Hennessee hadn't lied— and decided she would see if it rang any bells in Wolfe's steel trap of a mind.

Dear Ms. Oakes:

Washington! That's traitorous talk around here. Be at the picnic tables in front of the barn at six tomorrow morning. Expect to stay as long as you're needed. At the risk of being surly I'll tell you right now I'm not going to be responsible if you wrinkle the crease in your pants.

And for God's sake *don't* wear heels.

Regards,

Jonathan

P.S. I put your first letter up to the light and counted three typos. So there, smarty-pants.

Meg read the letter at least a half-dozen times and still didn't know what to make of it. She had the job! But would she be crazy if she accepted it? She could imagine explaining it to Wolfe. She was supposed to be playing bloodhound, not picking apples.

And what about this Jonathan McGavock? All right, the odds of his being Ross Greening were incredibly remote—all the more reason, at least from Wolfe's point of view, for her not to take the job—but he still might know the author.

She scowled to herself and knew looking for her quarry amidst the many orchard owners in the area had been based on dubious logic to begin with: Greening was a variety of apple, so maybe Ross had quit writing to go run an orchard. So if he hadn't, Meg could conceivably waste precious hours picking apples. When she'd left Manhattan, the two weeks Wolfe had given her had seemed like forever. Now she could feel the time slipping away. And she wasn't any closer to finding Greening than she had been when she rode into Rocky Springs.

She reread the letter. She was still Ms. Oakes, but McGavock also called her smarty-pants and signed his name simply Jonathan. The bit about surliness had her mystified. *He* hadn't been surly. His manager had. Unless . . . no. Why would Jonathan McGavock himself go through the aggravation of interviewing a swarm of teenagers—and one thirty-year-old?

She thought of the quick gray-green eyes flashing up at her from behind the desk and decided that the manager of McGavock Orchards wouldn't appreciate her having gone over his head to his boss. And undoubtedly she'd see more of him than Jonathan McGavock.

Did she really want to put up with the manager of an orchard grumbling at her? Hadn't she crossed enough men in power for a while?

For a lifetime, she thought. She couldn't take the job.

But what if the job could lead to a clue to the whereabouts of her missing author? So far she'd come up empty, and she didn't think she could put Wolfe off much longer. She would have to report back to him sooner or later. This was her first big assignment, however outrageous. She wanted to do it right.

There was just no choice: She *had* to take the job!

Her mind made up, she read the letter once more and wondered what would happen if Jonathan McGavock and his surly manager realized the closest she'd ever come to apple picking in her entire life was the other day, when she'd hit the pick-your-own stand.

"Ah, there's nothing to it," she told herself aloud and tossed the letter onto the pile with the others.

CHAPTER TWO

By noon the following day Meg had concluded that apple picking wasn't as romantic as it sounded, and Jonathan McGavock had revealed a streak of perversity when he'd agreed to hire her. Trying not to groan, she crawled up onto a boulder under one of the ubiquitous apple trees. To be fair, she thought, McGavock wasn't entirely to blame for her sore bones. Hadn't she herself revealed a streak of idiocy by getting up with the local chickens, wolfing down a skimpy breakfast, and showing up in an apple orchard with a half-dozen teenagers? *At six* A.M.!

During her long morning she had learned three things of relative unimportance: One, apple pickers were required to perform rather outlandish acrobatics; two, daily sessions in a Manhattan health club didn't necessarily prepare one for such outlandish acrobatics; and, three, brand-new jeans can cause blisters behind one's knees.

And here she thought she'd been so smart to go out and get herself a pair of jeans and sparkling new sneakers.

Letting her feet dangle down one side of the rock, she opened up the cup of homemade baked beans she'd purchased at the snack bar. She was feeling very sore, and very hungry, and very . . . no, not old. She sniffed the steaming beans and smiled. And then she laughed.

The word she was looking for was *refreshed.* Yes, in spite of all her mistakes and awkwardness, in spite of all her pain, she *had* enjoyed herself.

There was a rustle behind her, then a man's deep, amused voice: "Art told me you were wearing pink sneakers, but I didn't believe it."

Meg flew around, but already the subject of her curt letters to Jonathan McGavock was climbing onto the boulder. There was plenty of room, but she automatically slid over to the opposite edge, the top of her head brushing against an apple-laden branch. The manager of McGavock Orchards grinned. With a mix of pleasure and a sense of doom, Meg observed that he still had his dimples. And his shoulders. And the sun was highlighting the auburn in his mop of dark hair. Today's shirt wasn't flannel, however, but a dark green McGavock Orchards T-shirt with the big red apple logo. In desperation Meg had purchased one herself during her break: she had forgotten that cool autumn dawns often turned into warm autumn mornings, particularly when one was doing moderately strenuous labor.

Her mind raced: did he know about her letters to Jonathan McGavock? Probably he and his boss had had a chuckle over them. She wouldn't have been surprised if McGavock had hired her simply as a source of amusement for him and his manager.

Pink sneakers!

He was still grinning. "I guess that goes down as a surly remark, hmm?"

That obviously was an unrepentant reference to her first letter, which, just as obviously, McGavock had indeed shown him. Meg wasn't surprised, but, not wanting to alienate anyone, she tried to be pleasant. "But honest."

"Oh, I am honest, Ms. Oakes. That is one thing you don't have to worry about. You like pink?"

"It's amusing." She flexed her toes and offered a view of her size six-and-a-half powder pink running shoes. She wasn't about to admit to him that she hadn't owned anything pink since the age of four. "Cheerful, don't you think?"

He shrugged. "So long as they work."

"I haven't fallen out of a tree yet."

"Not for lack of trying, from what I hear."

She gave him a sharp look. "Now, *that* was a surly remark."

"But honest," he said, laughing.

"You're a blunt man, Mr.—"

"A cantankerous Yankee," he amended. "Are you finished for the day, or are you going to pick this afternoon?"

Meg refused to acknowledge her weary bones and picked at her baked beans. The teenagers had worked until seven thirty, then headed off to school, to return at three or so. That had left Meg pretty much in charge of an entire end of the orchard. When she'd gone off to buy her lunch, she'd run into two professional fruit pickers and learned they were rapidly making their way through another section of the orchard. She assumed they were being paid more than minimum wage for their efficiency and wondered why Jonathan McGavock had bothered at all with his swarm of fumbling, laughing—if energetic—teenagers . . . and her, of course. The former PR executive in pink sneakers.

"Six hours is enough for me," she admitted, his honesty prompting the same from her. "I'm going home to take a nice hot bath."

"Bubbles?"

"You are imaginative as well as cantankerous."

"And you're sore, Ms. Oakes. Ready to quit?"

He reached an arm toward her, and having no idea what his intentions were, Meg almost leaped off the rock. But before she made a complete fool of herself, he plucked an apple from above her head and bit into it. The inimitable crunch of a truly fresh McIntosh followed.

"Nope," she replied. "I want to earn enough to buy at least a full week's groceries."

He laughed. "I'm not sure apple season will last that long—unless you're a light eater."

"I won't be if I keep working this hard."

"The catch," he said, biting into his apple again.

Meg was beginning to like this surly character. Wolfe also possessed that peculiar brand of blunt honesty that made some people want to shrivel up and others want to slap him. Meg had found Wolfe's crankiness engaging from the moment she had walked into his office for her interview and he had said, "I'm hell to work for."

Wolfe . . . Ross Greening! *Oh, blazes,* Meg thought, *why did I have to think of those two now?*

But she wasn't supposed to be lallygagging in an

apple orchard with a handsome man . . . a cantankerous one or not. She wondered what rocks she was going to look under that afternoon for the reclusive writer. None, probably. It seemed to her she'd looked under every rock in western Connecticut, and all she had for her efforts was lower back pain and an apple picking job. She'd already decided this was her last chance. If she couldn't get a line on Ross Greening at McGavock Orchards, she was going to have to return to New York empty-handed.

"You were hoping I'd fall off a ladder, weren't you?" she asked idly.

"Or get stung by a bee or scream at the sight of one of nature's slimy creatures crawling up your arm. No such luck. However, you've never picked apples before, Ms. Oakes, and don't bother defending yourself. Even if it was fifteen years ago and in Washington, you'd have had to remember something. As it is, be glad I'm not paying according to productivity." He grinned again, pointing his apple core at her. "You'd end up owing me!"

"Be glad *you're* not paying—" Meg frowned. Then she sighed and looked over at the man stretched out so comfortably on the boulder next to her. "Oh, blast it all. You're Jonathan McGavock, aren't you?"

He bowed slightly, the impertinent twinkle back in his gray-green eyes. "At his surliest and most unprofessional, Ms. Oakes."

"You didn't have to hire me, you know."

"Ah, but I consider it a *compliment* that you applied for work at my orchard."

"You're going to rub it in, aren't you?"

"But of course."

With a devilish smile he pitched his apple core down the hill. Meg half-consciously watched the play of the tanned muscles of his arm.

"Would you compliment me again by staying to sort apples up at the barn?" he went on. "Art will show you the process—unless, of course, with all your 'experience' apple picking in Washington . . ."

He was being surly again. And cantankerous. Meg threw *her* apple core, but the damned thing had the audacity to drop at least a half-mile shy of his. She had planned to spend the afternoon tracking down Ross Greening, and she owed Wolfe an update. What she should do, she thought, was tell Jonathan McGavock that she didn't appreciate his sarcasm and she was going home. Probably he would fire her, but that wasn't like getting fired from a real job.

"You look very pensive, Ms. Oakes."

She glanced up and caught his half-smile. If she left in a snit, she'd never see Jonathan McGavock again. And for some reason, she wanted to. He interested her.

And maybe, she told herself, he would know something about Ross Greening. Maybe staying was the right choice for *both* her jobs—the one picking apples and the one hunting a missing author. And perhaps the right choice for herself.

"You're rationalizing," she muttered.

"I beg your pardon?"

She smiled sweetly. "Nothing. Of course I'll stay. And it's Meg, not Ms. Oakes. You call everyone else around here by their first names, don't you?"

"Ah, but they aren't ex-PR executives, and they don't give a merry damn how many typos—"

"You've made your point, Mr. McGavock."

He looked at her, and she almost choked at the intensity and life in those gray-green eyes. "Jonathan," he said simply, bowing slightly. Then he slapped his jean-covered knees and hopped down off the boulder. "See you around, Margaret T."

And he was off.

Two hours later Meg parked her Honda behind the Rocky Springs Free Town Library and thought that at that moment she wanted nothing more out of life than a warm bath, a good book, and a comfortable chair on her half of the library porch. But she knew that once she stopped moving, she'd be done for the day. Nothing would pry her from her lounge chair. So she trudged on over to the post office and checked her box. There was an envelope postmarked in New York but with no return address. Inside was a three-by-five index card: "Are you alive or has RG caught up with you? Call me *at once*. MW."

"Cute, Wolfe," she muttered and waved at Mrs. Hennessee, who was watching from the postal window.

Even waving hurt.

Thinking Wolfe was right and she should have bought herself some espadrilles and come as a suburban housewife, Meg walked over to Granger's. She smiled at bald-headed Mr. Granger behind the meat counter and, with as much subtlety as was possible, used her Wolfe Literary Agency calling card to place her call to New York.

Wolfe's secretary put her through to him immediately.

"Oakes? I was just about to call out the National Guard. Where the hell have you been?"

She glanced down at her broken nails and dirty hands. The blisters behind her knees stung. "Picking apples," she admitted.

"Apples!"

She could almost see the white-haired man of thirty-nine barking into his telephone. "It seemed a good way to get into the mainstream of life around here," she explained, "and Greening *is* a variety of apple—"

"He's a writer, Oakes, a writer. He is *not* an apple." Wolfe exhaled loudly. "Well?"

"Well what? That's all I have to say."

"Report!"

"There's nothing to report."

"You've been gone over a week! Dammit, you have to have something to report!"

Meg glanced around to see if anyone else in the quiet market had heard Wolfe's bellow. Mr. Granger smiled at her when she caught him staring. "I'm at a pay phone," she said, hoping Wolfe would take the hint. "When I have something substantial to tell you, believe me, I'll be in touch. It would help immensely if I could have a real name—"

"Impossible. I told you already."

It galled her no end that Wolfe knew Ross Greening's real name and refused to tell her. That, he maintained, would be unethical. How that same man could send out an associate to track down a writer who never wanted to see him again made no sense to Meg, but she had learned quickly that Michael Wolfe had his own very clear-cut ideas of what was and wasn't

37

ethical. And what he would and would not tell an associate.

"I know," she said, "but if you could just check the phone book—"

"I did. He isn't in it. Probably an unlisted number."

"Or maybe he's not within a thousand miles of here—"

"He's there, Oakes. You just have to flush him out."

Since she'd already argued ethics and lost, she didn't bring up the subject now. Instead she tried a subject she hadn't quite exhausted. "You might have better luck if you came out here yourself—"

"We've been over this before. If I show up, Greening'll run the other way or try to kill me. And I want to know what I'm getting into before I commit myself. If he's taken up banging tambourines naked in the town square, I want to know."

"But—"

"Find him, Oakes."

Wolfe hung up. Meg smiled at Mr. Granger, whom she was sure had heard her every word, and promptly ordered two steaks she didn't want.

She'd never find Greening. How could she? What Wolfe was asking was impossible. Outrageous. Beyond anyone's capabilities. She had been doomed to failure from the beginning.

So she put Greening and Wolfe out of her mind and took her aching body back down the street. As she trudged up to her apartment she unexpectedly found herself wishing she had someone she could cook the steaks for . . . or, better yet, with. And then, out of the blue, she thought of Jonathan McGavock. He would enjoy a nice grilled steak and a Waldorf salad and . . .

And what was she thinking? The man ran an orchard in the middle of nowhere. He wouldn't know an option clause from a wormy apple. He had nothing in common with her or her life.

He didn't appreciate her pink sneakers.

Ignoring a disturbing vision of his astute gray-green eyes, she shoved the steaks in her ancient refrigerator and told herself that Mr. McGavock was nothing but a big, handsome lug.

A little voice told her she couldn't be more wrong, but she stifled it and headed into the bathroom.

After her bath Meg went down to the library and browsed. The Rocky Springs Free Town Library had every one of Ross Greening's books. None was autographed. And, as Meg already knew, there were no pictures of the author on the dust covers. Just to see what would happen, she chose her favorite and checked it out. The librarian didn't say a word.

"I wish Greening would write another book, don't you?" Meg said.

"I don't read thrillers," the part-time assistant librarian replied with manifest disinterest, "but he is very popular."

"Yes." On an impulse Meg asked, "May I borrow your phone book a second?"

She could and did: there was no listing for Mc-Gavock, Jonathan.

Meg kicked off her sneakers, propped her feet up on the rail next to a box of geraniums, settled down on her half of the library porch, and began to read.

Greening's writing was just as crisp as she remembered, his plotting just as complicated, his pacing just as breakneck. Disinclined as she was to track him down, she did appreciate his skill as a writer.

She was engrossed in the third chapter when something brushed up against the ball of her left foot. Flipping the page, she wiggled her toes and hoped, rather absently, that whatever had lighted would fly off. It didn't. She scowled and wiggled harder. "Get lost, bug."

"Am I that offensive?" came a deep, familiar voice.

Meg's head shot up. "Mr. McGavock!"

He inclined his head politely and leaned against the porch rail. Now Meg could definitely define what rubbed up against the ball of her stocking-covered foot as a male hip. A decidedly solid, jean-clad male hip.

"I'm sorry," she said. "I thought you were—"

"A bug," he supplied.

"Well, yes. I didn't see you."

"Quit while you're ahead."

She smiled. "Okay, I will."

He didn't slide over to give her room, and she didn't move her foot—mostly because there was no place to move it. Her feet were neatly squashed between the geraniums and some seventy-four inches of Jonathan McGavock. Uncrossing her ankles and sitting up straight would only tell him just how conscious she was of her left foot and, more to the point, what it was touching. She didn't want that. She wanted—had—to keep her distance from everyone in Rocky Springs and the immediate vicinity. One of the chief reasons Wolfe had hired her was that she was known for being tenacious and thorough. "You're like a horde of grasshop-

40

pers," Wolfe had told her. "You don't leave anything behind." It had taken Meg a moment to realize that he was complimenting her . . . and that he was right. She'd come to Rocky Springs to find Ross Greening. And it would be precipitate of her to assume that Jonathan McGavock knew nothing about the reclusive author or, for that matter, that he would approve of her mission.

Until she knew beyond the shadow of any of Wolfe's doubts that he was the innocent orchard owner he appeared to be, Meg wanted to seem casual and cool and above suspicion . . . and unswayed by hard, jean-covered male hips.

But what was McGavock doing here? *Stopping by the library, of course.* Well, then, he could get on with it, she thought and smiled up at him. "Nice seeing you, Mr. McGavock."

He didn't move. "So you do live above the library."

"Of course." She batted her eyes with feigned coyness. "Would I lie?"

He paused, not hesitating, but looking at her pensively, as if he'd expected a different reaction. Then he said, all too seriously, "I have a feeling, Margaret T., that yes, very definitely you would lie."

She shrugged and shut her book. "What an ignoble thing to say."

"You'll find I'm not always a noble man."

"I think I already have," she said without animosity and stood the book up in her lap. She could see him glancing at the title. "Ever read any Ross Greening?"

Had she imagined that the muscles in his hip had tensed? If she rubbed her toes just under his belt . . .

She stopped herself in time: *Really, Margaret,* she thought.

Jonathan was giving her a cool, very controlled smile. "Yes, as a matter of fact. I thought his first book was all right, but the next two fell short somehow."

"I disagree. I think he's shown a deeper and broader talent with each successive book."

"Do you?" he said enigmatically.

Meg was starting to picture herself as a bug being stuck to a light bulb by some sadistic twelve-year-old, so she dropped her feet to the porch floor, sat forward, and yawned. "Don't let me keep you," she said, hoping he would take the hint. "I'm sure you didn't stop by just to check whether I'd lied about where I live."

"Oh, but I did."

"You've got to be kidding! A woman fibs about her age, and now you don't believe a word she says—"

"*And* fibs about her work experience and probably one or two other things as well."

She waved a hand. "Details."

"Maybe, but let's just say I'm wondering if with you two and two add up to four."

"Why should they have to?"

He crossed his arms over the apple of his Mc-Gavock Orchards T-shirt and gazed frankly at her. But Meg, lately of New York City, was used to frank gazes. She wondered what he thought of the cotton drawstring pants and raspberry silk kimono top she'd changed into. Wolfe would have been disgusted, of course, because they were eye-catching and rather sophisticated, but Meg was comfortable.

And McGavock couldn't have cared less. "I guess I'm just curious. It's not every day an ex-PR executive wanders into town, rents an apartment above the library, and takes a job picking apples."

The dubious way he said "ex-PR executive" made her wonder if he even believed that much about her. It was one of the few truths she'd told him. "I'm recuperating," she said, not defensively.

"From what?"

"From being a PR executive," she replied and silently, pointedly, and very soundly cursed Michael Wolfe for putting her into the position of having to lie to begin with. Now she had to keep on lying. She leaned back in her chair and hoped she looked comfortable. She wasn't. "I'm enjoying the restorative powers of fresh air and hard work."

"Apple picking isn't hard work, Margaret T."

She was beginning to like the way he said Margaret T. "Honest work?"

"For some," he said.

"Is that another surly remark?"

"I don't know," he said, unfolding his arms and easing himself off the rail. "Maybe. Guess I'll get out a book now that I'm here." He paused, looking down at her. "Libraries can be tough on an author's royalties, though, can't they?"

Meg laid the Ross Greening on her lap and said with careful equanimity, "I wouldn't know."

His eyes held hers for an awkward moment, and then he smiled cheerfully. "Right."

Sarcastic remarks rose to her lips. Defenses. Offenses. Questions! But Meg pulled her lips between her teeth and said nothing. For once she would leave well enough alone. For once she wouldn't be too thorough or too tenacious. She took some satisfaction in turning

43

around and watching him open the screen door to the library, but she didn't succeed in making him feel awkward. He tossed her a final half-amused, half-challenging glance and went in.

At least she'd shown him she was undaunted by his doubts, and should by some freakish chance he actually know why she was in Rocky Springs, keeping her mouth shut and trying to bait him had made her look innocent. Or at least *reasonably* innocent.

But how could Jonathan McGavock possibly know she worked for Wolfe? How—

"Your guilty conscience is making you jumpy, Oakes," she muttered to herself.

Through the screen door she saw McGavock engaged in conversation with the librarian and thought to herself: *He's disgustingly good-looking . . . but let him be just an innocent apple grower.*

The thought—nutty as it was—that he could be Ross Greening made her spine crawl. Impossible! Wolfe would be crazy to send her after a man like that! No. Greening was a nice, normal, decent fellow.

But did nice, normal, decent fellows have eighty-stitch scars on their thighs and impressive physiques?

No, men like Jonathan McGavock did.

With a shudder Meg grabbed her sneakers, tucked her book under her arm, and padded quickly up to her apartment.

Jonathan McGavock was not Ross Greening!

"These are all the copies we have," the assistant librarian said, handing Jonathan four issues of *Publishers Weekly*. "We throw them out after a month or so."

Jonathan thanked her and took the stack to a reading table. He hoped Meg was watching. He hoped she was trembling in her stocking feet. He just knew he was right. He flipped to the people section of each issue of the trade magazine.

The third one had the item he was looking for.

He almost whooped but settled for a grim smile. So his memory hadn't been playing tricks on him. A Margaret T. Oakes had recently been hired by Michael Wolfe Literary Agency in New York.

And a Margaret T. Oakes had just been hired by McGavock Orchards in Connecticut.

Coincidence?

"Not likely," he muttered and checked out the damning issue.

With a burst of energy he pushed open the screen door. He had every intention of dropping the magazine in Meg's lap. And that would be that. She'd explain what the hell she was doing in Rocky Springs, or he'd haul her back to New York and dump her in Wolfe's office and make *him* explain.

But her lounge chair was empty, her pink sneakers gone. Jonathan's entire body tensed. What was the blasted woman up to? He'd have her head—and Wolfe's too!

Then he smelled the steak cooking and heard the classical music playing.

And he thought of Meg perched in an apple tree, arms and legs stuck out in four different directions, awkward but determined. He couldn't help it. He liked the shape of her lean figure and the way her eyes looked past him when she lied. And she *had* lied to him. There was no question of that now.

In spite of everything, though, an evening with Ms. Margaret T. Oakes held a certain allure for him. He considered trotting upstairs and inviting himself to dinner . . . *and handing her the incriminating magazine?* He growled softly in aggravation and reconsidered. Maybe he shouldn't rush this. Maybe he should handle this situation in his own way . . . and in his own good time.

CHAPTER THREE

At five the next morning Meg rolled over and muttered, "The thrill is gone." She could hear crows cawing outside her window. Getting up with them the first day had been unpleasant but adventurous. The second day was unmitigated torture and far from adventurous. Muscles she hadn't heard from in years were announcing their presence and begging her not to move. She groaned and thought to herself that Wolfe wouldn't care if she stayed in bed. Jonathan McGavock wouldn't either. He'd—

"He'd *expect* it."

She slowly, painfully crawled out of bed. Picturing his smug face if she didn't show up for a second day of apple picking motivated her to move toward the bathroom.

" 'Apple picking isn't hard work, Margaret T.,' " she mimicked, stepping under the stream of hot water.

After her shower, ten minutes of stretching, three cups of coffee, and a monstrous breakfast, Meg had at least stopped groaning out loud.

Not until she was puttering along the back road to New Rocky Springs did she remember McGavock's strange comments the afternoon before on the library

47

porch. He knew something about Ross Greening. She was sure of it! But was he just automatically suspicious of strangers, or did he have a reason to think she had come to town to track down Greening? Maybe—

She broke off the thought. *Ifs, ands* and *buts* weren't going to get her anywhere. No amount of speculation would give her the answers she needed. She'd have to call Wolfe and tell him she had a clue and his name was Jonathan McGavock.

But would it be nice—more ethical, anyway—to talk to McGavock first? Be up front with him about her reasons for coming to Rocky Springs?

Wolfe would kill her.

As she rolled into the McGavock Orchards parking area she shoved aside her confused, garbled thoughts and decided she'd figure out what to do about her apple grower with the gray-green eyes the next time she saw him.

"Good ol' seat-of-the-pants Oakes," she mumbled to herself and joined the group of teenagers.

But Jonathan McGavock didn't surface under any of Meg's apple trees the entire day. All her sense of self-satisfaction for even having gotten herself out of bed went for naught, and so did all her half-baked plots for worming out of him what he knew about her elusive author. And there was, to her surprise, a vague, indescribable feeling of disappointment. Had she actually been looking forward to seeing her surly Mr. McGavock?

Art Pesky, the manager of the orchards, caught up with Meg as she was climbing into her Honda to head back into town. He was an efficient-looking, wiry little man well over thirty, but Meg doubted that his age got in his way or anyone else's. "There you are," he said. "Jonathan wants to see you up at the house." He pointed to the rambling farmhouse across the field. "He said he'd be out back."

Meg didn't know whether or not to panic, so she saved herself the bother. She'd be cautious instead. "Any idea what he wants?"

"Nope."

"I should go right now?"

"Yep."

"Art . . ." Her voice trailed off as she paused to think about whether she was being cautious or dumb. If McGavock wasn't already suspicious of her, asking too many questions now could rekindle his interest in her lies. And then what?

"Yep?"

She closed her car door and chewed on her lower lip. "Mr. McGavock . . . Jonathan . . . are the orchards his only source of income? I don't mean to be nosy—"

"You're new in town," he said, as if that explained everything. "Jonathan's main business is forest management. The orchard's more or less a hobby."

"A hobby? I see. Um—thank you."

A hobby, she repeated to herself and started across the field toward the farmhouse. Forest management! Before selling his first thriller Ross Greening had spent eight years in the employment of the United States Forest Service.

Impossible!

But things just didn't feel right in her bones, and six hours climbing trees wasn't the only reason.

The farmhouse was white with black shutters, probably close to two hundred years old. Two huge maples in the front yard were just beginning to hint at the yellow and orange they would turn in a couple of weeks. Marigolds and pansies blossomed in the flower beds, and there was a large stump, probably of an American elm, on the other side of the dirt driveway. A Labrador retriever was collapsed on the front lawn. Meg went around back. A little red tractor and a decrepit Land-Rover were parked side by side in front of a blue shed. Behind the shed were two stacks of wood: one unsplit cordwood, the other split cordwood. Between the piles wielding a massive ax was Jonathan McGavock.

Meg didn't announce herself at once but stood watching as with remarkable ease he split one hunk of wood after another. The ax would go up, there'd be a second's pause while he took aim, and then down it came. *Crack!* The defenseless chunk of wood would fly off in two different directions.

He didn't seem the least bit startled at seeing her when he leaned the ax against the shed. "I'd have made a good executioner back in Henry the Eighth's time, don't you think?"

"Cheery thought."

He grinned, little bits of wood and sawdust clinging to the sweat pouring down his temples. "Old Henry did have a rather final way of dealing with his enemies," he said.

"Not to mention wives."

"Same difference."

"My, my, aren't we cynical today."

"Not just cantankerous?"

"Both. You could use some sweetening up."

He grabbed a chamois shirt from atop the woodpile and wiped his sweaty face. "What would you suggest?"

She shrugged, wondering why her heart was pounding so hard. Probably just lack of sleep combined with too much physical labor. A sweaty, dirty woodsman wasn't about to give her palpitations. And, she reminded herself, she was supposed to be on her guard. This very same sweaty, dirty woodsman could also be a writer who'd sold millions and millions of books. Or, more likely, *knew* something about Wolfe's missing author.

So why was she noticing his shoulders and his eyes and every drop of sweat on his face, and the way his T-shirt clung to his muscular chest?

"I don't know," she said finally. "A cold glass of cider?"

"You're an optimist, Margaret T. I need one hell of a lot more than a glass of cider. It's been a long day."

She wanted to ask why, but for no reason at all—except maybe the twinkle in his eyes—her heart had begun to beat even harder and faster. It was time to change the subject. "Art said you wanted me."

Jonathan grinned. "Now you're talking, Margaret T. Just how sweet are you?"

"I'm not known for being sweet at all."

"Ah," he said, his grin fading to a delicious smile. "A tart?"

"Adjective, not noun. If we were comparing me to an apple—"

"You'd be ripe for the picking?"

"I'd be as tart as a cooking apple." She looked right at him and forgot all about being cautious. "Say a

51

greening." He didn't bat an eye but merely slung his shirt over his shoulder. "My tart tongue separated me from my last employer, you know."

"Well, maybe it'll endear you to your current employer. I like tart apples myself," he said, his voice growing husky as he moved toward her, "and tart tongues. . . ."

Leaving his shirt draped over one shoulder, he settled his big hands on Meg's hips and smiled into her eyes just as he lowered his mouth to hers. She could smell the wood dust and the sweat and the tanginess of the autumn wind on him, taste them on his lips, but when his tongue stroked the corners of her mouth and mingled with hers, all she could taste and feel was the masculine heat of his body. And it was enough.

"Nectar," he breathed, pulling away much too soon, "pure, sweet nectar."

She blanched at the cocky gleam in his eyes and the even cockier spring to his step. He'd kissed her, she'd kissed him. Oh, blast, she thought, how was she ever going to broach the subject of Ross Greening? She'd promised herself she wouldn't lose her objectivity, and yet she could feel it slipping away. Wolfe would not be pleased. And when he learned the truth about her, neither would Jonathan McGavock . . . whether he knew anything about Ross Greening or not. Because she *had* lied to him and probably, given the opportunity, would be compelled to lie again.

Trying to regain some measure of composure, she put a hand out toward him. "Jonathan . . ."

He wiped his face with the sleeve of his chamois shirt. It was navy blue. *Of course,* Meg thought. He slung it back over his shoulder and winked down at her. "Maybe your tongue's not as tart as you think, Ms. Oakes."

"I didn't mean physically!" she blurted, exasperated. Where was her sharp and sarcastic tongue? And she almost groaned aloud as she thought: *Recovering from the most magnificent kiss I've had since I don't know when.*

"You didn't?" he said, amused.

"Of course not. That was a figure of speech. I wasn't leading you on, Jonathan McGavock. I—*Quit grinning at me!*"

"Why? You're funny." His grin broadened, and he crooked his elbows and bent back his shoulders, stretching. Then he added, "Sweet."

"I am not sweet!"

"I think you are. Cider?"

He was maddening! If only he would stop grinning, she thought, she might be able to deliver some withering comment and walk away. No: stalk off. But he didn't stop grinning, and she wondered if he'd enjoyed their kiss as much as she had. "What did you want me for?"

"To sweeten me up, of course. I've been in a bear of a mood all day."

She scoffed, not believing him. "Do I get paid extra?"

He stepped jauntily past her toward the back steps of the house. "Sarcasm will get you everywhere, Margaret T." He opened the door and motioned chivalrously for her to enter. "A tart tongue produces the sweetest kisses—"

"Stop!"

He laughed. "The lady doth protest too late."

With a frustrated groan she stepped past him into a small mudroom filled with more kinds of work boots than she'd ever imagined existed, well worn jackets, more chamois shirts, slat baskets of various sizes, tools, and junk. There was an open doorway into the kitchen. The walls were a cheerful yellow, and there were a stove and refrigerator that would have been the envy of many restaurants, and jars of freshly canned tomatoes and applesauce on the counters, and a bushel of apples on the floor. A fat furry white cat was sleeping in the middle of a giant pine table.

"Impertinent creature," Jonathan said but didn't shoo him off.

"This is nice," Meg said in an attempt to radically change the subject. But she wasn't lying. It *was* nice. Homey and comfortable. Not at all the sort of place in which one would expect a famous writer to hole up. She was feeling better. Maybe her days of fruitless searching had made her paranoid. She smiled at Jonathan. "Do you live here?"

"Most of the time."

Oh, curses. "Meaning?"

"Meaning I like to get away occasionally."

So what was suspicious about that? "Then you have no kids and no wife?" Ross Greening, she remembered, was single. Wolfe had claimed there wasn't a woman alive who could put up with his former client. But, Meg admitted to herself, she'd asked the question not just for research purposes but because she wanted to know if Jonathan McGavock, innocent apple grower or not, was attached.

He set two tall glasses on the counter next to the refrigerator and scowled at her. "Be a hell of a thing to

54

be kissing one woman while I had another lurking about."

"Yes, I suppose it would."

"And there aren't any kids. I've never been married."

"Oh."

"You?"

"No."

He took a jug of cider out of the refrigerator and filled the two glasses while Meg sat wondering how she hadn't managed to radically change the subject after all. They were back talking about themselves.

She tried again. "Art says you do forest management."

"Whatever that means," he said, laughing. "Mostly it means I own a lot of land and tell myself and quite a few other people around here how to manage it to the best advantage of the environment and their pocketbooks." He handed Meg a glass of cider and sat opposite her with his glass. "It's not all that glamorous, I'm afraid, but I'm my own boss."

"I'd like to be my own boss someday," Meg said absently. "Do you do your own cutting?"

"Sometimes, but most of it I contract out."

She just couldn't help it. She had to ask: "Then you've used a chain saw?"

"Of course."

"Ever been wounded?"

His eyes rested on her for a moment, and then he sipped his cider. "Once. That's all it takes. I was careless—and lucky."

She waited for him to go on and tell her the gory tale, but he just sat quietly drinking his cider and petting his cat. *Wolfe would press him,* Meg thought. *No, he wouldn't! He'd know if Jonathan McGavock was also known as Ross Greening.* This was ridiculous! She'd call her employer the second she got to town and tell him she'd found a likely candidate for his accursed author.

But would she be betraying a man who had kissed her? Violating a trust somehow?

Wolfe wouldn't care. He had sent her to find Greening, and he wouldn't care how she did it or who she used in the process. As he had said, "Greening's a gold mine, Oakes; I want him." And therefore she, as Wolfe's associate, should want him too. At any cost.

"Something wrong, Meg?"

"No, unh-uh. I was just thinking about chain saws. They give me the creeps."

"You just have to know what you're doing and avoid mistakes, that's all." He paused. "I would think a country girl from Washington would know that."

"Oh. Yes, well, I guess I would if I was from Washington."

"You're not?"

She didn't need to look at him to know he was being smug again, but she did anyway and saw the gleam in his eyes. He had already known she had lied. "I grew up in a small town north of San Francisco," she admitted, not lying. "I went to college in the East and ended up staying out here."

He looked at her with mock horror. "You mean you lied to me, Ms. Oakes?"

"A white lie. I wanted the job."

"Why?"

There was nothing smug or mocking in his expression now. He wanted to know. She shrugged and tried to smile. "I'm not sure you've earned an explanation, Mr. McGavock."

"I hired you, Meg." He smiled. "And kissed you."

"That's not enough—"

His brow quirked in amusement. "Oh?"

She nearly choked on her cider. "That's not what—Are you always this exasperating?"

"Incisive and alert, Margaret T.," he corrected. "It's what keeps me going."

"Speaking of which, I should be heading out." She rose and started for the door. "Thanks for the cider."

"Not even going to stay and find out what I asked you up here for?"

She couldn't stop a cocky grin. "Not if you keep being incisive and alert."

He laughed. "One point to the woman in the pink sneakers. All right, I'll be honest with you. I asked you up here to find out if you wanted to ride with me to New York tomorrow."

She turned, giving him a blank look. "New York?"

"As in city. Manhattan. Skyscrapers, Broadway—"

"You're going to New York?"

"Yes, I do that every now and then. I shower and shave and put on clean clothes, and off I go."

"Why would you want me to go? I mean, why would I want to go? There's nothing—I don't have anything to do with New York."

He leaned back in his chair, looking very calm and very much in control. Incisive and alert. "I thought you were an ex-PR executive."

Meg found herself thinking once again about flies

57

being stuck to light bulbs, but she replied steadily, "I am."

"But not in New York?"

"Hartford," she lied. "I worked in Hartford."

"Oh. My mistake. For some reason I thought you had worked in New York." He smiled and tipped his glass toward her. "Must have been the heels. Only a New Yorker would show up for an apple picking job in heels, don't you think?"

"Obviously not. Well, I—I've got to go. Thanks for the invitation, but no. I—" *I'd better quit while I'm not too far behind!* "Good-bye."

She pushed open the door, and she could see him stretched out on the chair, absolutely and perfectly in control of the situation. He called out nonchalantly, "The invitation still stands, Meg."

"Sorry, but no," she said hurriedly, "I—you don't pay me enough for me to be able to afford trips to New York."

And she fled, hoping he wouldn't think of anything else to say before she was out of earshot. He didn't. All she heard as she raced across the field was the roar of his laughter.

Meg stood in front of the pay phone next to the meat counter debating whether she should call Wolfe. She had only to mention the name Jonathan Mc-Gavock to Wolfe and she'd know. Wolfe would gulp or curse or do something to give himself away. Most likely he'd be cool. He'd say something like: "I think you've had enough fieldwork for a while, Oakes. Why don't you come home?" And she'd go back to Manhattan and discover that Wolfe was going to be out of

58

the office for a few days . . . in Connecticut, trying to come to terms with an author who'd told him and the publishing world to take a hike.

If he wasn't Ross Greening, no harm done. Maybe Jonathan knew Greening, and maybe he didn't, but at least there was a fighting chance that she could get through to him and explain the whys and wherefores of her presence in Rocky Springs. Why she wanted to explain and wanted him to understand was another subject, another problem, and one she would encounter in the privacy of her apartment, not standing at a meat counter.

If, however, Jonathan McGavock *was* Ross Greening . . .

"There's the rub," she mumbled to herself.

She caught Mr. Granger staring and smiled innocently. Didn't people in Rocky Springs talk to themselves?

She sighed. But what if he *was* Ross Greening and Wolfe decided to take her into his confidence? She tapped her lips with her index finger. "And then what?"

Wolfe would want to know everything his associate and his number one author had said to each other.

"And done?"

To be sure.

Mr. Granger leaned over the counter. "Can I help you, miss?"

She laughed self-consciously. "Oh, no, no, I was just thinking out loud. I can't remember if it's oregano or dill I'm out of."

"Spices are in aisle two."

Thanking him, she meandered over to aisle two.

The telephone wouldn't go anywhere while she pondered her dilemma.

What would Wolfe do when he found out she was picking apples at McGavock Orchards—whether or not the owner knew or was Greening? She hadn't been subtle—or successful—with her lies. She hadn't even used an alias! What would Wolfe do when he found out she and Jonathan McGavock had actually interacted, and now she was worried he might be her quarry?

"If you think you've found Greening," Wolfe had instructed her on that memorable day in New York, "don't go near him. Call me. Even if you're wrong. I don't want him to see you—if it can be helped."

"What if it can't?" she had asked.

"Lie. I don't want you alienating him." Wolfe had given a rare grin. "You let me do that."

Meg hadn't envisioned finding Ross Greening at all. From the start she had figured it was some sort of initiation rite Wolfe put new associates through. But he was quite serious. When she finally had forced herself to look at the problem realistically and creatively, she had come up with the apple angle. This particular corner of Connecticut was crawling with orchards. And since she was supposed to be looking for a writer named Greening who had worked for the United States Forest Service? Of course that would be the place to start. Her plan had been vague at best: She would get into the orchard crowd as an apple picker and nose around. She had never expected to confront any orchard owners or certainly any potential Ross Greenings.

She had meant to avoid any potential Ross Green-

60

ings . . . as Wolfe had instructed. Just a line on Greening, that was all she'd wanted. Then she would call Wolfe and let him take over.

And instead here she was fairly bursting with the memory of having *kissed* a potential Ross Greening!

She could hear Wolfe now: *"You what?"*

How could she explain? "He was all sweaty, Mr. Wolfe, and he has dimples and gray-green eyes. . . ."

It wouldn't matter if she'd found Greening or not: Wolfe would fire her on the spot.

And Jonathan McGavock, if he was indeed Ross Greening, would run her out of town.

"Which leaves me between a rock and a hard place," she mumbled and bumped into a woman buying olive oil. "Oh, excuse me. I talk to myself when I grocery shop."

The woman gave her a look that said loud and clear that any woman in pink sneakers and a green Mc-Gavock Orchards T-shirt could be expected to talk to herself any time of day or night.

Meg grabbed jars of oregano and dill, for what purpose she couldn't imagine, and headed toward the check-out counter.

She had to find out if Jonathan McGavock and Ross Greening were one and the same on her own. Somehow. Without jeopardizing their budding friendship or her job and, she hoped, without having too many more people in Rocky Springs and the vicinity end up thinking she was some kind of lunatic.

On her way out she smiled and waved at Mr. Granger.

When Jonathan had finished laughing, he went into the front room and grabbed the Rocky Springs Free Town Library copy of *Publishers Weekly* off the coffee table. He didn't bother sitting down but simply flipped the magazine open to the page he'd dog-eared and re-read the announcement: "Margaret T. Oakes, former publicity director for book packager J. T. Hood, Inc., has joined the Michael Wolfe Literary Agency as an associate."

Michael Wolfe Literary Agency was in bold print.

Jonathan grunted and pitched the magazine across the room. "Hartford, my hind end!" he muttered. "Insurance!" He stormed out the front door. "The little sneak," he grumbled. "The miserable liar!"

Ordinarily, of course, he wouldn't have remembered a short item from a trade magazine. He wasn't that interested in the comings and goings in the publishing industry. But he *was* interested in anything that happened in the Wolfe agency, and he made a habit of going down to the library every few weeks and scanning *Publishers Weekly*. When Jonathan had seen the despicable name in bold print, naturally he'd paid attention.

And remembered.

Margaret T. Oakes.

He'd been suspicious the second she'd walked into his office and he'd raised his eyes, just for a second, and seen the outfit she was wearing. Rarely—never, in fact—had anyone applied for an apple picking job decked out the way Meg, Margaret not Megan, Oakes had been. Heels, for God's sake! And a Viyella shirt! He had pegged her as a phony right then and there. The only question was whether she was from the press or a publishing house or just a free-lancer. Clearly *someone* had tracked him down. He hadn't considered Wolfe, not then. Wolfe, the only person in publishing who knew Greening's real name, would have had the easiest time finding him of anyone, and surely he could have come himself. He owed Ross Greening that much.

But the sniveling coward had sent an associate!

Little Miss Margaret.

Jonathan hadn't made the right connections until she'd sent him her snippy letter criticizing his interviewing techniques. Seeing the name and the heading and—

"Of course!"

He had the sweet little lady now. He raced back inside and plucked the first of her letters out of the rolltop desk in his living room.

And there it was.

Centered beneath her name on the top of the page was an address in a neat, crisp, no-nonsense type: West End Avenue, New York, New York.

He couldn't wait to see her try to wriggle out of this one!

Letter in hand, he took long, purposeful strides back out onto the porch. He paused to pinch off a wilted geranium blossom . . . and remembered the touch of Meg's foot on his hip yesterday afternoon . . . the heady burning sensation that had gone through him . . . the thoughts and imaginings that had awakened him periodically throughout the night. . . .

And he remembered the kiss that hadn't been part of his plan . . . her wide, golden eyes . . . her warmth.

Was it possible she didn't already know who he was? Was it possible Wolfe was using her?

Jonathan knew he should be angry. He had guarded his privacy for a long time, occasionally going to extraordinary lengths to keep his identity as Ross Greening from overlapping with his identity as Jonathan McGavock. Even when he had done a rare author's tour, he had managed to deflect interest from his real name and even avoid photographers. It wasn't a cause with him. It had just happened that way.

Then people began to realize that Ross Greening was just a pseudonym and that no one knew the author's real name—as if somehow it made a difference. *Not* knowing whetted their appetites. They didn't simply want to know; they *had* to know. Which only made Jonathan more stubborn about keeping his private life separate from his life as Ross Greening.

Wolfe had been characteristically unsympathetic: "Look, McGavock, you're not a goddamn woodsman anymore—you're Ross Greening."

Jonathan, however, had been reluctant to let the man he was die and someone else rise up in his place. He liked being able to retreat into the woods and be the anonymous face he'd always been. And, of course, there was the issue of Ross Greening and his writing; of *Jonathan McGavock* and his writing. The irritations of the impending invasion of his privacy and the pressures of what he wanted to do with his work combined, and he disappeared. It had been remarkably easy, and remarkably fulfilling.

And now here was Margaret Oakes on some nincompoop mission from Wolfe. Jonathan was back on the merry-go-round again. The life he'd fashioned during the past two years was in jeopardy. He should be angry!

But he wasn't. From the very beginning, anger hadn't played a role in any of his plans. And he didn't know why. Was it Meg, he thought, or himself?

He tossed the wilted blossom into the flower bed below the porch and trotted off to his Land-Rover. There wasn't a glimmer of anger inside him, just curiosity and determination . . . and a certain feeling of exhilaration. Maybe it was time to end the months of seclusion. He had known he would someday—but on his terms, not Wolfe's. He would write the books he wanted to write and be the man he wanted to be. Wolfe and his lovely emissary would just have to live with his terms.

And he'd be damned if they were going to get away with sneaking into his world and coercing him back into theirs. Jonathan was a step ahead of Wolfe this time. *And* his charming and delectable cohort. Their timing wasn't the best, but he could work things out. They were going to learn a few things about Jonathan McGavock, aka Ross Greening. And, he thought as he climbed into his Land-Rover, he was going to have a hell of a time teaching them . . . and especially Margaret T.

CHAPTER FOUR

Meg had planned to spend the rest of the afternoon in her apartment thinking up ways out of her mess, but she stopped at the library to return her Greening novel. Mrs. Babcock, the head librarian, mentioned that she'd heard Meg was picking apples at Mc-Gavock Orchards. Meg acknowledged that she was and commented, "It's a gorgeous orchard, don't you think?"

"Oh, yes, isn't it?" Mrs. Babcock said. "Jonathan's done such a beautiful job up there. No one thought the orchards could be brought back after Gertie Lundstrum let them go for so long. Not that it was her fault, of course. There was no one around to help her after her husband died, and she was already up in her seventies by then. I think she'd be tickled at what all Jonathan's done in such a short time."

"She's dead, then?"

"A little over two years. She had two children, but they don't live here in town, so they decided to go on and sell the place."

Meg swallowed hard. "And Mr. McGavock bought it?"

"Paid cash, from what I hear," Mrs. Babcock said,

lowering her voice. "And then he came in and just turned the place around. Heaven only knows how much money he's put into it. Just converting that old barn must have cost a fortune."

And Jonathan McGavock, if he were Ross Greening, would have a fortune. Meg tried to sound nonchalant as she said, "I never would have guessed he had money."

"I know what you mean."

"Do you know where he's from?"

"New York, I think. He doesn't talk about himself much, and we don't like to be nosy in this town."

"Of course."

Meg didn't explain that ordinarily she didn't like to be nosy either, but she was tracking down a best-selling author and her boss had told her to ask questions. "People tell anything to a woman in espadrilles," Wolfe said, on what authority only he knew. Instead Meg excused herself and looked over the shelves of new releases. Since the library had formerly been a private residence, the rooms were small and cozy with the flavor of both library and home. There were no "stacks" to speak of, but every available space was filled with books and shelves, and signs in each room urged patrons to ask at the desk to order books not in the library. It was so different from the libraries in New York Meg was used to, and yet nonetheless still a library.

As she scanned the various titles her mind was racing. Jonathan McGavock had moved to Rocky Springs two years ago. Ross Greening had made his exit from the literary world two years ago. Jonathan McGavock had money. Ross Greening had money.

Meg wondered if there was any discreet way she could ask Mrs. Babcock if she'd ever seen Jonathan McGavock in a pair of shorts and noticed a scar on his thigh. "His inner thigh," Wolfe had told Meg, adding perversely, "Came close to ruining himself, he told me." Meg had calmly asked Wolfe how in God's name she was supposed to get a look at Ross Greening's inner thighs. "You're not, but you could always ask around town," he'd said blithely, and Meg had had no idea whether or not he was serious. She had quickly changed the subject.

Wolfe. She wished she hadn't thought of him. She had all the clues she required for a quick, possibly damning phone call to New York. Not making it was taking a huge risk, but she had warned Wolfe that his harebrained scheme could come to no good end and—

Blast it all, why had she ever agreed to do Wolfe's dirty work for him? Greening would return to the literary world in his own good time. Or he wouldn't. There were just some things Michael Wolfe couldn't control.

Pity he didn't realize it, she thought.

Small children in overalls, droopy pants, and crookedly buttoned sweaters started filing in for the Friday afternoon story hour, distracting Meg from her unpleasant thoughts. One little girl had picked a geranium for Mrs. Babcock.

And towering above the last straggler walked Jonathan McGavock with a peck of apples tucked under one muscular arm. "Hello, Margaret T.," he said cheerfully and then followed Mrs. Babcock and the little troop into the children's reading room. He returned without his peck of apples.

"Such a big ogre you are," Meg said.

"Have to keep up appearances, you know."

"I thought you'd be on your way to New York by now."

He eyed her closely. He had thought the prospect of his going to New York would have signaled that he was on to her and put the fear of God in her, but apparently not. She looked as cool and steady as ever, which made him wonder what *would* put the fear of God in her. "I changed my mind," he said affably. "I decided I could accomplish more by staying here—at least for now."

"Oh, I see. I guess this is a busy time for an apple grower."

He smiled, amused. Didn't she have any idea at all that he wasn't sticking around because of his orchard? Art Pesky could handle everything there. Jonathan wanted to handle his thirty-year-old apple picker. Or try. "I guess," he replied, noncommittal.

"I've decided to work tomorrow," she said abruptly, not liking the look in his eyes. Or, more truthfully, liking it too much. It made her remember his mouth on hers. It made her consider possibilities she couldn't afford to consider. And it made her stomach twist and churn.

He was glancing at the Ross Greening book still on Mrs. Babcock's desk. "You got through that pretty quickly," he said matter-of-factly.

Meg wasn't sure she appreciated the change of subject, but she attempted a lighthearted and innocuous response: "Oh, I devour Greening."

"Do you, now?"

She looked up sharply, but he was straight-faced. A

well-timed chorus of giggles emanated from the children's room. So much for innocuous! Or was she just paranoid, reading meanings into idle comments that just weren't there?

Mrs. Babcock returned, and with an inscrutable smile Jonathan handed her an envelope. "One copy please," he said, "and it's confidential."

Meg had learned how to take a hint. "It's nice seeing you, Mr. McGavock," she said politely, as if their kiss had never taken place. It shouldn't have, after all.

"Likewise, Ms. Oakes."

As she turned she caught the amused twinkle in his eyes. He wasn't pretending their kiss had never taken place! If he was just a good-looking apple grower and forester, he probably thought her behavior somewhat peculiar. Skittish. Absurdly naïve. If he were Ross Greening, he probably thought—what? The same, likely enough.

Instead of leaving at once Meg wandered off and pored through shelves of books. She wasn't looking for anything in particular. She wasn't *doing* anything in particular. She simply couldn't bring herself to creep up to her apartment just yet.

And why not? she asked herself.

Simple: because Jonathan McGavock was still here. "So?" she muttered, half-aloud.

So she was doing her job. Wolfe wanted to find Ross Greening, and Meg was supposed to exhaust every lead. And Jonathan McGavock was her most promising lead.

"And I'm a liar," she mumbled with a sigh.

She could hear the children laughing across the hall. They sounded so happy. Their contentment somehow only seemed to accentuate Meg's frustrations, her questions and misgivings. And her loneliness. She listened, smiling to herself. She liked Jonathan's world. She didn't belong in Rocky Springs—not permanently —but she liked it. And maybe he didn't belong here permanently either. What would happen, she wondered, if the people of Rocky Springs discovered Ross Greening lived in their midst? Probably nothing. Connecticut had more than its share of the rich and famous. Maybe Rocky Springs didn't, but Meg was betting they'd be blasé about it all: "Ross Greening lives here? How nice."

A few minutes later she heard Jonathan saying good-bye. She waited, wondering if he would hunt her up, but she heard the screen door open and close, and sighed deeply, tired and confused. Was she relieved or was she disappointed that he hadn't said good-bye? She didn't know. And that, she thought, was the worst part.

She *had* to find out for sure if he was Greening!

Ha! How much proof did she need? She had more than enough circumstantial evidence to take to Wolfe.

"But I can't," she said and quickly grabbed a book by another of Wolfe's clients.

When she returned to the front desk, the children were filing out, with McIntosh apples clutched in their little fists.

She smiled to herself: what could a man who passed out apples to small children possibly do to her?

If he was Ross Greening and didn't want anything to do with Michael Wolfe . . . everything.

When she went out onto the porch, Jonathan was there, leaning languidly against the rail, handsome and

71

insolent and unexpected. Meg found herself suddenly in a good mood and was surprised he had so great an effect on her. She put aside the thought and said, trying not to sound too cheerful, "I thought you'd gone home."

"I had to run by the post office for a minute. What're you reading now?" He turned his head sideways and glanced at the title of Meg's latest selection: a novel by Alicia Moores. He smiled to himself; he'd met Alicia at one of Wolfe's client Christmas parties a few years ago. Meg Oakes wasn't being particularly subtle, he thought. Of course, neither was he. "I was wondering if I could interest you in dinner—if you're not too exhausted."

Meg blinked, pleased but wary. "Why?"

"All the usual reasons," he said with a shrug and added quietly, his eyes gleaming, "and then some."

She decided he didn't intend for her to take him seriously. "Such as?"

"Your golden eyes, your delicious laugh, your—"

"You're laying it on a bit thick, McGavock."

"You don't believe me, Oakes?"

"Nope. You couldn't possibly know if I have a delicious laugh."

"I can guess, can't I?"

"Sure, if you want."

"I want."

"Somehow I don't think you trust me, Jonathan."

"No? After all the white lies you told me, why shouldn't I trust you?" He reached out and chucked her under the chin. "Come on, Meg, laugh."

"You haven't said anything funny."

"Have I said something wrong?"

He didn't sound the least bit contrite. In fact, Meg thought, he sounded as if he *wanted* to do something wrong—to set her on edge or something. It was as if he knew exactly who she was and was toying with her. The way a cat toys with a mouse before giving it a final lethal swat.

"You're scowling, Meg."

"Jonathan, are you—" She stopped herself in time. Just coming out and bluntly asking him if he was Ross Greening was her style, but she wasn't working for herself. She was working for Wolfe. "You're trying to aggravate me."

"I'm trying to make you laugh."

"I thought you were trying to get me to go to dinner with you."

"That's what dinner's for."

"What?"

"Making you laugh." He grinned broadly and added, "Deliciously."

Meg hid a sudden weakness in the knees by leaning against the railing on the other side of the geraniums. "I didn't know you were a romantic, Jonathan," she said as coolly as she could.

"There's a lot you don't know about me, Margaret T.," he said, suddenly serious.

"And is that what dinner's for too? I'll find out more about you, and you'll find out more about me?"

"If that's what you want." He smiled enigmatically. "Tempted?"

Maybe dinner would do it. She could hang out her dirty laundry, and he could hang out his. Of course, his wasn't necessarily dirty. Could he help it if he was Ross Greening, and Wolfe had sent her to track him down? *Wolfe!* What would he want her to do? Call and update him. Ask for instructions.

Run!

"Holy moly," she said, well under her breath.

"Was that a yes?"

She smiled graciously. "Why not?"

"You could sound a little more enthusiastic," he grumbled.

"You want enthusiastic? Okay." So she popped off the railing and went down on one knee before Jonathan, one hand on her heart. She actually batted her eyes. "Oh, Jonathan, Jonathan," she breathed, trying not to ruin her performance by laughing, "I would be so honored, so thrilled and delighted, so overcome with joy and gratitude if I could have dinner with you."

Jonathan looked over her head and said with a smug smile, "Hello, Mrs. Wilson."

Meg swiveled her head around and saw the woman who'd caught her talking to herself over the oregano at Granger's Market stepping onto the porch. She glanced down at Meg, then smiled noncommittally at Jonathan and said hello. Mortified, Meg watched the woman dart into the library.

She leaped to her feet and glared at Jonathan. "Don't you *dare* laugh, McGavock."

"Laugh? Me? Why, Meg, you've ruined my reputation," he said with mock horror.

"Yours! What about mine?"

"You don't have one around here." He gave a mischievous grin and added, "Yet."

"Very funny," she said, but he only grinned more broadly and more mischievously and trotted nimbly

74

down the porch steps. She called after him: "Where are you going?"

"Granger's—to buy dinner."

"But I thought . . . Aren't we going to a restaurant?"

He turned around, walking backward, the late afternoon sun dancing on his hair. Meg didn't know when she'd met a more dashingly attractive man. Probably never.

"Who said anything about restaurants?" he called back. "I said I wanted to have dinner with you. I didn't say I'd take you out to dinner."

"You cheap Yankee!"

He laughed. "Better watch yourself, Margaret T. Rocky Springs is full of cheap Yankees. You'll get run out of town yet."

"But I was just kidding—"

She spun around in a circle to see if anyone was around to have heard her. Mrs. Babcock and Mrs. Wilson were in a discussion at the desk just inside the library. Except for Jonathan the sidewalks were empty. But who was listening at windows? Half the town probably.

She started to defend herself further, but Jonathan was already on his way past Mrs. Arnold's flower bed. Meg could hear him chuckling. And suddenly terror struck at her heart: what if he meant to have dinner *in her apartment?*

"Oh, God."

Taking the steps two at a time, she raced upstairs. What act of idiocy had she just committed? She couldn't have Jonathan McGavock up to her apartment! Even a completely unsuspicious person would notice at least some of the little signs that she was *not* an ex-PR executive from Hartford. And Jonathan Mc-Gavock was hardly unsuspicious. He would see everything, he would demand an explanation, and he would know she had lied.

Well, so? she thought. That was one way of getting the dirty laundry out into the open. Maybe it was better that way.

She remembered his kiss and Wolfe's instructions and decided no, it wasn't better that way. For a while —just until she could get her thoughts together—she had to continue with her charade. The most intelligent thing she could do right now, she thought, was to meet Jonathan downstairs and refuse to let him into her apartment. And if he insisted, she would just have to be firm and cancel dinner.

Which would only make him more suspicious.

And, besides, she *wanted* to have dinner with him. The prospect of spending another evening alone in Rocky Springs did not thrill her. The prospect of spending an evening with Jonathan did. It was that simple. The complications were elsewhere. So she scrambled around her tiny apartment and hid all the evidence and hoped for the best. If he gave her an appropriate lead, she would tell him everything.

"But if he looks under the couch cushion, I'm a goner," she muttered and raced back down to the porch.

Unless, of course, Jonathan *wasn't* Ross Greening. But even then, she thought, she had lied to him about her background and her reasons for being in town. She sighed as she collapsed onto the lounge chair on the porch, and a disturbing thought struck her.

Did she *want* Jonathan McGavock to be Wolfe's missing author? A best-selling writer instead of an apple grower and forester? Did it matter? She wasn't sure, but when he ambled onto the porch with his bag of groceries and his dimples, she knew she wanted nothing more than to spend the evening with him. Evenings alone in New York after a hectic day were one thing, but out in the country they were quite another.

But she wondered if evenings alone would ever be the same again after tonight. Jonathan McGavock was walking into her life and her world, and she wasn't so sure *she* would ever be the same again. With a tightening of the knot in the pit of her stomach, she acknowledged that right then he was the only person she wished to be with.

And naturally he insisted on having dinner in her apartment.

"Still no telephone?"

Jonathan handed Meg a plastic bag of fall snow peas and watched her shake her head and pivot quickly on her heels. Too quickly. She hadn't liked his question.

"I'm working on it," she replied, dumping the peas in a colander.

"You didn't bring a phone from your old place?"

"Nope."

"If you have your own equipment, all you have to do is call the phone company and have them flip the right switch."

"I'm aware of that."

Testy. He smiled and tapped her on the shoulder with a loaf of Italian bread. She reached around and took it. "They still charge an arm and a leg for flipping a switch, though, don't they?"

As he expected, she seized the proffered excuse. "Yes, they certainly do! It's expensive enough as it is to set up in a new apartment."

He handed her the mushrooms. "Especially if you're maintaining another apartment as well, I would think." *Zap,* he thought, *now I've got her.*

She cocked her head around at him and grinned, not the least nonplussed. "And picking apples at minimum wage for a living."

One round to you, Margaret T., he thought and set the chicken breasts, yogurt, and white wine on the counter. The kitchen was small but adequate and, like the rest of the one-bedroom apartment, starkly decorated. It had come furnished, so he couldn't blame Meg for the abominable taste in slipcovers and rugs or the gold gilt wallpaper in the bathroom. But the naked walls? The tables and chests devoid of knickknacks and clutter? So far he had seen nothing more personal than yesterday's newspaper.

She blanched when he opened up a cupboard and found nothing but all-natural peanut butter, oregano, and dill. "Old Mother Hubbard went to the cupboard," he said.

She snatched the cupboard door from him and shut it hard. "I'm still getting settled."

"Brought along all the necessities of high living, I see," he mused. "Do you eat oregano and dill for breakfast?"

"I just felt like buying them."

"Oh, but of course."

On the pretense of chilling the wine he pulled open

the refrigerator and found it was somewhat better stocked with yogurt, milk, orange juice, butter, and McGavock Orchards oatmeal bread. "No jelly to go with the bread and peanut butter? Horrors."

"I survive."

He smiled briefly. "Perhaps."

"What's that supposed to mean?"

"What do you think it means?"

"I think it means I was crazy to invite you up here."

"You didn't invite me, Meg. I invited myself."

"So you did."

"Regrets?"

She looked up at him and smiled. "No."

He leaned against the refrigerator and watched as she lined up the ingredients he'd bought on the counter. By the way she moved he could tell she was still stiff from picking apples, but there was a natural grace to her movements, an agility and mystery that made him want to know more about the real Meg Oakes. In spite of what he knew about her already, she was becoming so elusive . . . almost ethereal.

Impulsively he brushed his fingers across her hair just above her ear. She whirled around in a start, and he dropped his hands to her waist, smiling as she looked up at him in question. "So you are real," he said. "I was beginning to wonder. You seem so impermanent, Meg. I feel as though you're here with me one second and gone somewhere else the next . . . or maybe not here at all."

"That's funny," she said softly, settling into his arms, "I've been thinking the same about you."

"Why? I have a telephone, a house, furniture, junk that's been piling up for years."

"Yes, but . . ." She looked up at him, into the depths of his gray-green eyes, and he could feel her probing his soul. "Somehow I sense that's only a part of who you are . . . or maybe not who you are at all. I don't know you, Jonathan. I look at you, even now, and realize I don't know you at all."

"Do you want to know me?"

"Yes."

He touched her lips gently with his. "That's what tonight is for," he said and kissed her again, lingeringly this time, until he could feel the ache rising in him and the stiffness in her lower back as she tried to control the ache in her. Reluctantly he ended the kiss. He looked at her, into her golden eyes, and knew that he hadn't lied, and neither had she. Tonight they were Jonathan and Meg . . . not Ross Greening and Michael Wolfe's associate. Just a man and a woman and everything they could be to each other.

Putting aside his suspicions and misgivings, Jonathan took charge of the kitchen and sauteed boneless chicken breasts in butter and made a sauce of sliced mushrooms, yogurt, and white wine. Meg steamed the snow peas and heated the bread. It was a simple meal, and they spoke little. Jonathan would catch her eyes on him and smile. And then he would be watching her, and she'd notice and smile too. Part of him wanted to talk and tell her all about the man who'd become Ross Greening, but another part of him just wanted to be there in the little apartment with a beautiful woman who intrigued him as none other had in a long, long time, and let everything else be for a while. It hadn't been his plan, but, then, he was beginning to realize that plans were impossible where Margaret T. Oakes was concerned.

They had the rest of the wine with their meal and afterward coffee, which Meg insisted on making herself.

"You've already done more than your share," she said, not on her guard, "so just sit and relax a minute."

A little voice warned her that wasn't what she wanted to say, but she couldn't remember why, so she ignored it. But as she filled the coffeepot with water she could see Jonathan lowering himself to her couch, and suddenly she remembered. Tulsa! Beneath that particular cushion she had stuck a seven-page story outline, three chapters, and a cover letter addressed to her at the Wolfe agency from an author in Tulsa. "Don't take anything incriminating!" Wolfe had decreed. And at her own peril Meg had chosen to ignore his advice. She tried not to wince. At least with the water on she couldn't hear the crunching of papers. She hoped he couldn't either.

And she had *promised* herself she wouldn't let him sit down! Have dinner, she had told herself, and get rid of him.

So instead she'd told him to go in and sit down and relax! She was making him coffee!

She was doomed.

She brought a tray with the coffee and cups into the living room, where Jonathan was sitting cozily on the couch. The woman from Tulsa, Meg thought, would likely not be pleased about her scrunched-up manuscript. Meg set the tray on the Formica-topped coffee table but didn't sit down immediately.

Naturally Jonathan noticed her hesitation. "Aren't you going to sit down?"

"Hm? Sure. Of course, I—"

Where had she put Wolfe's notes on Ross Greening? Wolfe wanted them back, intact no doubt, and he'd warned her to memorize everything so she wouldn't have to take the file with her. She had memorized everything, but she'd still taken the file with her. And hidden it . . . under her pillow! Of course. She passed him a mug and took one to her only easy chair. She plopped down.

Crunch! She feigned a smile. "Whew, what a day."

"What was that?"

"What was what?"

"I think you sat on something."

The complete guide to New York literary agents. "Oh, it's just the springs. You never know what you'll get when you rent a furnished apartment."

Jonathan was looking pensive and concerned, as if someone from his little town had cheated her and he didn't like it.

"I don't mind," she said quickly. "I mean, it's fine until I decide whether to move here permanently or not. I—" She stopped. "Jonathan, what are you thinking about?"

"I'm trying to think whether I know anyone on the library board. You should at least have a decent chair—"

"Oh, my God!"

"What? Meg, is something wrong?"

She recovered quickly, coughing. The library board knew she was Margaret T. Oakes from West End Avenue, New York, New York. Jonathan McGavock didn't. She preferred to keep it that way. If only she'd been more circumspect! Wolfe would have littered half of Connecticut with aliases.

"No, nothing," she said quickly. "Something went down my windpipe." She coughed once more and smiled. "There. Please, don't mention me to the library board. They've been very decent about rent, and I don't mind the chair. Honestly." She smiled again but didn't suppose she was very convincing. She added smoothly, "It's nice of you, though, to think of me."

He smiled, amused. "I haven't done much of anything else since you marched into my office." He patted the cushion beside him. "Come, Meg, and sit beside me. I want to talk to you."

She was swallowing hard. The space under that particular cushion was occupied by a twenty-page story outline, three chapters, and a cover letter to Michael Wolfe himself from an author in Daytona Beach. *Oh, Lord, what have I done?* she thought and didn't move.

"Meg?"

"I think I'm falling asleep," she said lamely. "I got up so early. All this fresh air. I guess I'm not used to it."

She yawned for effect, but her miserable look was real. He was the most interesting man ever to come her way, and for the sake of her job she had to get rid of him. Why the hell didn't she just *ask* him if he was Ross Greening? Hadn't enough happened between them that he would at least listen to an explanation?

Not if he was Greening, she thought. *She* wouldn't listen to any explanations if she were Greening herself! And besides tonight was loaded with too many other things. She was too distracted by the sexual tension between them and the emotions Jonathan aroused in her to explain coherently and convincingly her role in Wolfe's scheme.

"I'm sorry, Jonathan," she said sincerely.

"Don't be sorry," he said with such understanding she felt even more miserable. He rose and came to her, taking her by the hands and lifting her to her feet. "Come on, love," he said, "I'll tuck you in—"

"No!" She went rigid in his arms but forced herself to relax and be calm. Where were her wiles? Where were her wit and sarcasm? Melting, she thought; melting right here in Jonathan McGavock's arms. "Why don't we go for a walk?" she suggested, not wanting to let him go but not daring to lead him into her bedroom.

He gently brushed his knuckles along her chin and the line of her jaw, smiling, holding her about the waist with his other arm. "You'll end up riding me piggyback, and as much fun as that might be for me, I don't think the town elders would approve." He kissed the tip of her nose. "Change your mind, Meg, and let me tuck you in. I won't stay if you don't want me to, but let me love you a little."

"I can't. I have a rule about going near bed with a man on a first date. . . ."

"Is that what this is? A first date?"

"I don't know. Yes, I guess so, but—No, I don't guess so. Jonathan, you have me so confused!"

He let her go and said, not entirely sympathetically, "I think you have yourself confused, Margaret T."

"Jonathan, nothing about us is ordinary. Haven't you noticed? Of course this isn't a date! Dates are ordinary. This is more like—oh, I don't know what. A test. A game. We don't trust each other, Jonathan, and maybe—" She took a deep breath: *if Jonathan doesn't slaughter me, Wolfe will.* "Maybe we shouldn't."

The gleam in his eyes only added to the overall effect of his smirk. "Are you trying to tell me something, Meg?"

"I think I'm trying not to tell you something, Jonathan. I—I just need some time to think things over."

"Meg—" He sighed. "All right, think things over, but remember, no matter what, I want to see you again. And I'm not easily put off."

"Does that mean you'll understand if I haven't told you everything?"

"Meg, I *know* you haven't told me everything, but I want to see you again."

He smiled and touched her hand, and she tried not to acknowledge the little sparks that brief contact ignited all through her but was forced to acknowledge them anyway. "Okay."

"If I can't tuck you in, the least I can do is give you a good-night kiss."

He scooped her into his arms and brought his mouth down onto hers, not giving her the chance she didn't want to push him away. Her mouth and tongue greedily took everything he offered and begged for more. Her lean, tired body stretched against him, felt his energy and the hardness of him in his arms and legs and torso. In his mouth she felt only his gentleness and sensitivity.

The little sparks turned to great roaring fires, and she couldn't think. She could only feel and wonder and respond.

"If I don't go now, you won't be able to get rid of

me," he breathed into her mouth. "What do you want me to do, Meg?"

Stay!

But she didn't speak aloud. A thought intruded. If he stayed, she would find out if he had a scar on his inner thigh. She would know at last if he was Ross Greening, and her despicable mission would be over. If he stayed, too, he would find the evidence of who she was there under her pillow . . . and they might never get to his scar. They might never get beyond her duplicity.

Somehow it was wrong. She didn't want to find out who he was in bed, and she didn't want him to find out who she was in bed. There had to be more honesty between them first. More trust. More openness.

But what if he's not Ross Greening? He won't give a damn about Wolfe's notes on Ross Greening!

She couldn't take the risk, and it still didn't change anything. She *hadn't* told him everything. She needed time to think, and the courage to explain.

"I don't think I've ever had a good-night kiss quite like that one," she said, smiling.

"But good night?"

"Good night, Jonathan."

He smiled and winked and left without another word.

Through her open window Meg could hear him whistling merrily as he went to his car.

Jonathan sat for a moment in the quiet darkness of his Land-Rover. Meg had excited him as no woman ever had. God, he wanted her! And he didn't give a good solid damn *what* Wolfe had put her up to. That just didn't enter into it. Nevertheless, Jonathan did wonder what the little liar had under her pillow that she didn't want him to see. A picture of Michael Wolfe? Business cards?

He chuckled to himself, starting the Rover. While she'd lingered in the kitchen to put away the last of the dishes they'd done together, he'd found the Tulsa proposal under the couch cushion. It had been all he could do to keep from thrusting the thing under her nose.

But he *would* get the truth out of Margaret T. Oakes. There was no question about that. There was only, he thought, a question about timing . . . and results. He wanted more than answers from Meg. He remembered the feel of her slender body against his, the play of her tongue in his mouth, and shuddered with longing. "A lot more than just answers," he said aloud and drove off.

CHAPTER FIVE

When the crows woke her at dawn, Meg rolled over and tried to go back to sleep. Jonathan McGavock would have to truck on down to town with a backhoe to get her to his orchards today. She was going to rest. Do errands. Enjoy autumn in the country. Have a little peace and solitude. *Plot.* She needed a plan of action. She needed to quit thinking about Jonathan's eyes and mouth and all the wonderful possibilities of a romance with him. Which was impossible and unrealistic—whether or not he was that accursed wayward author she was tracking down. They were just too different. He wasn't the sort of man at all she liked to imagine sitting across from her every morning at the breakfast table. He grew apples, for heaven's sake. He farmed trees and wielded an ax.

He was also sexy and gorgeous and absolutely thrilling to be around . . . and she was a damned fool for thinking about him in any sort of permanent terms! Why not just enjoy him?

"Because I *can't!*" she groaned, burying herself under her pillow.

Clearly her nerves were shattered and it would be wise to avoid Jonathan McGavock for now. She needed a day of peace and solitude. Under different circumstances apple picking might have been the perfect retreat, but she was afraid Jonathan would park himself under her tree and make remarks about crunchy couch cushions and tucking her in and such. He would ask more questions she wanted to answer but didn't dare. And she would have to bite her tongue to keep from asking the one question she longed to ask: *Are you Ross Greening?*

Or maybe she'd just blurt out the truth and see whose head rolled. It was the not being able to predict what she would do when she saw Jonathan next that was driving her crazy. Wolfe had put his most outspoken associate into a situation that required discretion. She was having to play her cards close to her chest, and she didn't like it. She wanted to toss them on the board and see who had what.

Sleep eluded her, so she finally gave up tossing and turning and made herself a breakfast of toast and apple butter. Her apartment seemed lonely. Her *life* seemed lonely. She almost wished she'd gone apple picking after all. She sighed, disgusted with her own uncertainty, and got herself cleaned up and dressed and went out to do errands.

The Rocky Springs Historical Society was having a bake sale in Mrs. Arnold's driveway, so Meg bought a lemon meringue pie and a mum plant and was surprised to learn that several of the women knew her name. Probably they were on the library board, she thought. Or they knew someone on the library board, who'd passed the word about who'd taken the apartment above the library, and—

Did they all know she was from New York? If word

was out, then possibly Jonathan had heard, or would hear, and she'd be caught in yet another lie.

Which was bound to happen sooner or later.

She walked over to the post office, pushing the door open with her back so as not to risk tipping the pie. The bottom was still warm. She set it and the mum on the counter in the middle of the tiny post office and opened up her box.

A McGavock Orchards envelope was tucked between a one-page mimeographed circular for Granger's and a notice that her box rent needed to be paid. Mrs. Hennessee was watching. Meg smiled as she tossed the circular and the notice into the trash, grabbed her pie and her mum, and with the envelope stuck in her back pocket, left. How soon would word get around that the new woman in town had flushed at the sight of a McGavock Orchards envelope in her postal box? What if she and Mrs. Babcock at the library and the woman who'd caught Meg talking to herself over the oregano all got together and compared notes?

Oh, so what? Meg thought to herself. But she was a city person. She wasn't used to having strangers take an interest in her private life.

It was all she could do not to drop the pie in the middle of the sidewalk, announce to the whole damned town that she was on the prowl for Ross Greening, and tear open the envelope and read aloud whatever was inside.

Realizing that was the kind of mood she was in reaffirmed her decision not to go apple picking.

Her pace quickened as she headed upstairs to her apartment, and she almost lost the pie. But she forced herself to slow down and managed to get herself, the pie, the mum, and the letter into her apartment intact.

She tore open the envelope, unfolded the letter inside, and stared.

It was a copy of her first letter to the owner of McGavock Orchards. The one she'd typed in a fit of pique on her personal stationery.

With her West End Avenue address printed so crisply and elegantly beneath her name.

The entire heading was circled in black ink, and beside it was a note in a singularly arrogant scrawl: "Oh, what a tangled web we weave. . . . J."

The cool, level-headed businesswoman in her said to make a pot of tea, have a piece of pie, and think. The angry, impetuous woman in her said to take the damned pie out to McGavock Orchards and throw it in the sneaky bastard's face.

She crumpled up the letter and threw it on the floor. "He knew all along!"

Yesterday afternoon in the library he'd had her letter right there in his hand. *That* was the "confidential" item he'd had Mrs. Babcock copy. And Meg had been standing right there! Why hadn't he confronted her with it?

Because then he wouldn't have been able to have his fun and games at dinner. He hadn't invited her to dinner to make her laugh! Had she laughed? No. And why not? Because Jonathan McGavock didn't care if she laughed or not. He'd toyed with her. He had wanted her to relax and learn to like him before he zapped her this morning with the letter.

"The snake in the grass knew all along I'd lied!"

She grabbed her car keys and bag, resisted toting along the pie, and stormed down to her car.

There was a crowd at McGavock Orchards. Cars from Massachusetts, New York, and Connecticut filled the dirt parking lot and lined both sides of the narrow paved road. Children were choosing pumpkins from among the hundreds spread out behind the picnic tables. It was a glorious autumn day, and the day-trippers were out.

Meg wasn't about to cruise up the hill looking for a parking place, so she screeched to a halt smack in the middle of Jonathan's driveway, blocking it. When she hopped out and circled around behind the car, she noticed the New York license plate and groaned at her own idiocy. Even if she hadn't sent McGavock a letter on her personal stationery, he was bound to have noticed her license plate sooner or later. How careless could she have been? *Hartford!* Why, why, why, she thought, had she lied?

And lied so abominably.

Wolfe, she thought. That was why. And her own quite reasonable fear of losing her first job after five months of unemployment.

Othello, the black Labrador, was asleep in the front yard, as usual. He didn't even blink when Meg stepped over him and banged on the front door. Fists clenched at her sides, she waited. She gave him thirty seconds before she knocked again. Then she gave him another ten seconds, and when he still didn't come, she stormed around back.

Cordwood was neatly stacked beneath a lean-to behind the shed, the pile of uncut wood gone, the ax nowhere to be seen. The chopping block sat innocuously amidst the wood chips and sawdust. Meg had to resist a vision of Jonathan wielding his ax, sweat pouring down his brow . . . and then his mouth on hers and his husky voice, teasing and seductive. Even now in the sweet, fresh autumn air, furious as she was, she could remember every detail of how he smelled and felt, and what he had stirred inside her.

She pulled her gaze sharply from the block and looked around. On the other side of the Land-Rover and the little red tractor was a black Porsche. Fast, sleek, expensive cars didn't impress Meg, but they did give her pause when parked in the backyard of an outdoorsman who, by budget and choice, shouldn't drive one.

So she paused and stared and thought: What woodsman would own a Porsche?

The answer was clear enough: one who's sold a few million books.

The screen door opened, and Jonathan stepped out and grinned at Meg. "Hi, there."

She glanced down at the leather suitcase in his hand and noticed the monogrammed *JM*. At this point, she thought, she wouldn't have been surprised to see an *RG*.

"Margaret T.," he said cheerfully, "I do believe you're speechless."

"Livid would be more accurate."

"You don't like my car?"

"I don't like your tactics."

He shrugged and dropped the suitcase into the back of the car. In spite of herself Meg couldn't take her eyes off him. He was wearing jeans, naturally, but she didn't think any man she'd ever met wore jeans the way he did. They emphasized the length and solidness of his legs and added to his overall image of rakish sexiness. Leaning against the Porsche, arms folded across his chest, hair blowing in the light wind, he looked calm and controlled and incredibly virile.

Meg decided she was just as glad she hadn't brought along her lemon meringue pie.

"You don't like my tactics," he repeated. "I see. Wouldn't you say this is a case of the pot calling the kettle black?"

"No. You didn't have to mail that letter, Jonathan. You could have showed it to me last night at dinner, and we could have discussed it."

He smiled. "I didn't want to give you indigestion."

"You've been toying with me, Jonathan."

"And you've been lying to me, Meg."

"Just a few little white lies! And what business is it of yours where I'm from? I do my job, and that's all you need to worry about!"

"Is it?"

"*Yes!*"

"Suppose I want to worry about more than how well you do your job?"

"You can't."

"Why not?"

"Because I don't want you to."

"Ahh." He shifted some, still unruffled. "And suppose I don't care if you want me to or not? Suppose I want to know everything there is to know about you? What then, Meg?"

"I leave."

He smiled, but she could see the cold resolve creeping into his eyes. "I have your address, remember? I can follow you."

She looked at him with all the steadiness she could muster. She had never met anyone as tenacious and determined and outrageously bold as he was. His tactics were on a par with her own! "I can move," she said coolly.

"You won't have time. I'll find you first."

"Is that a threat?"

"A simple statement of fact."

"I'm annoyed with you, Jonathan."

"And I'm annoyed with you."

"But?"

"But I still want to make you laugh, Margaret T."

She couldn't stop a smile, mostly because she didn't want to. "Deliciously?"

"Any way at all."

He pulled away from the car then and took her hands in his. She could feel his calluses against the tenderness of her own raw blisters. Soon she would have calluses too. He opened her palms into his and kissed the red places at the base of her fingers. "We'll make a country girl of you yet," he murmured and brought his mouth to hers.

It was a brief kiss but erotic and full of promise, and when it ended, Meg found herself not so much breathless as in a daze. She smiled dreamily as he stroked her chin. Her anger seemed such a dim memory. Had she actually thought this strong, gentle man capable of such deceit and arrogance?

"I want to know you, Meg," he breathed against her mouth. "I want to know all of you." He paused, tak-

95

ing a step backward. His eyes never left hers. "And I will."

"My being from New York doesn't matter?"

"I don't know. Does it?"

She licked her lips. "I did work in public relations, you know—for a book packager in New York."

"That's quite a ways from a Hartford insurance company."

"PR is PR."

He leaned against his car again. Wherever he was going, he didn't seem in a hurry. Meg tried to picture him in something more appropriate for driving a Porsche. To her surprise she could. Easily. His strong frame would look magnificent, and not at all incongruous, in all the bold, expensive, masculine clothes she imagined. But it also looked incredibly right in just jeans and a shirt. And perhaps no one but she would question that he should be driving a fast sports car. Why did she question it? Because she had to, needed to. Because if she didn't, she had not just to consider but to believe that he was more than her mountainman apple grower.

"And what do you do now?" he asked, his gaze direct, unflinching.

She smiled. "I pick apples for a sneaky man who doesn't trust me."

"Why?"

"Because I'm a glutton for punishment, I guess."

To his credit he didn't lose patience. "You know what I'm asking, Meg. Is there another job in New York?"

"I should hope so—lots of them."

"Why did you come to Rocky Springs? Just to pick apples?"

Wolfe's hold on her was weakening. She could sense it slipping out of her, oozing into the ground beneath her, and was powerless to call it back. She couldn't think of Wolfe and her job in Manhattan and the months she'd spent looking for another job, not just any job but the right job. The one she'd found. She wanted to tell Jonathan everything. Slowly she edged her way to the chopping block and sat down. How symbolic, she thought, looking at him. She still could feel the touch of his lips and tongue, the roughness of his cheek against hers, the promise of his strong, hard body.

"No," she replied at last, not looking away.

She half-hoped he would put words into her mouth and provide her with the excuse—the lie—that would have been so much easier, not just for her but, she thought, for him as well, but he didn't. He motioned to her with one finger and said calmly, "Go on."

"I'm also looking for Ross Greening."

He didn't tense at all. Either her statement meant nothing to him, or he'd been prepared for it. He merely pushed one foot out a few inches in front of the other. "The writer?" he said.

She nodded. "That's not his real name."

"Why?"

"I don't know. I guess he doesn't want people to know he's a writer."

"I meant why are you looking for him?"

"Oh." She shrugged. "So I won't get fired again."

"Again?"

"Mmm. Last time I bucked an order from on high,

97

I was 'outplaced'—in other words, fired. So this time I'm not bucking. I'm obeying."

"Am I to presume this Greening fellow doesn't want to be found?"

She stretched out her legs and made a design in the sawdust with her pink sneakers. "It's what I'm presuming."

"Then you're sort of like a bounty hunter."

"Sort of." She glanced up at him. "Do you know Ross Greening, Jonathan?"

"No," he said heavily, moving off the car. "No, I don't."

He snapped the driver's side door open and stuck one leg in, looking over the roof of the car at her. "I'll see you on Monday, Meg."

"Where are you off to?"

"New York."

"New York! But I thought—"

"What's the matter? Are you afraid I'll drive by your place on West End Avenue and discover something else about you you don't want me to know?" He patted the roof and winked. "Maybe Margaret T. Oakes doesn't exist."

"Why do I have the distinct impression you're changing the subject? We were discussing Ross Greening. Now—"

"We weren't discussing Greening," he argued. "We were discussing you. Greening just came up."

"Supposedly he lives around here."

"It's a nice place to live. Good-bye, Meg."

"Are you sure you don't know him? He was cut by a chain saw a few years ago. He has an eighty-stitch scar on one of his thighs. And he—"

"Meg, love, I don't go around checking out men's thighs. I'm sure if I'd stumbled across a world-famous thriller writer, incognito or not, I'd have remembered him, don't you? I don't know Ross Greening—certainly not the Ross Greening the world knows." He smiled. "Have a good weekend. Try not to think up any more lies while I'm gone."

She almost leaped off the block and offered to go with him but didn't. Perhaps the invitation was no longer open. And, even if it were, joining him would probably only lead to another disaster.

Because this time she knew *he* was the one doing the lying. Somehow, some way, Jonathan McGavock knew Ross Greening.

Meg took herself out to lunch at McGavock Orchards and indulged herself in an apple dumpling while she planned her next move. She came up with a hundred different possibilities, but they were all either unworkable or unethical. Or both. So she bought a bushel of apples and went home and made applesauce.

Two hours later she couldn't stand it anymore and headed over to Granger's Market. As usual Mr. Granger was stationed behind the meat counter. "Calling New York again?" he said cheerfully.

So much for secrets in a small town, Meg thought and flashed him a smile, giving a noncommittal half-nod. She turned her back to him and dialed Wolfe's home number. His message machine answered, so she hung up. Being a workaholic, Wolfe could be at his office. So she tried there.

He growled into the phone on the first ring. "Wolfe."

"Hi, this is Margaret—"

99

"Terrific."

She didn't like the mean, sarcastic note in his voice. "I wanted to warn you," she said, her knuckles turning white as she clenched the receiver. "I'm not sure what's going on, or if I'm right, or anything, but I think I might have found Ross Greening—or at least someone who knows him. He owns an orchard in New Rocky Springs."

"Does he?" Wolfe didn't sound surprised, just sarcastic and mean. "And when did you meet him?"

"Last week. I was sure he wasn't your man, though, or I'd have said something sooner." That wasn't exactly the truth, but she hoped it would work. "I'm not sure even now, but I think—well, he's in New York. I thought you'd want to know. Just in case."

"Then you've talked with him?"

"Yes, unfortunately. It couldn't be avoided."

"And you think he might be coming here to the office?"

"Or your apartment. He's—well, I don't think he's easy to put off."

Wolfe's voice became very quiet but still cuttingly sarcastic. "When did he leave?"

"This morning."

"And you waited until now to call me?"

If she squeezed the receiver any harder, it was going to break in two. "Yes."

He said nothing.

"Would you like his name? Then you'll know if I'm talking about the right man."

"Oh," he said, "you're talking about the right man."

"You're sure? But how do you know?"

"Because he's sitting here in my office with his god-damn size twelves on my desk!"

Meg sank against the cool glass of the meat counter. "Jonathan McGavock?"

Wolfe growled. "Ross Greening!"

"Then he is—Oh, no."

"You've done a hell of a job, Oakes."

She could see what was coming next. She'd been there before.

Wolfe scoffed in disgust, inhaled sharply, and then roared, *"You're fired!"* And hung up.

At least, Meg thought as she replaced the receiver, he hadn't offered any platitudes. He hadn't minced words. Michael Wolfe would never say "outplaced" or compliment her on her various skills and then knife her in the back. He preferred direct, frontal attacks.

You're fired. . . .

Succinct and to the point.

She attempted a smile at Mr. Granger and ordered a string of hot dogs. Then she went back to her apartment and fixed an early supper. Applesauce and grilled hot dogs. Delectable. She remembered the taste of Jonathan's chicken in white wine, yogurt, and mushrooms . . . the taste of his mouth on hers.

He wouldn't be any more thrilled with her than Wolfe.

She rinsed off her dishes. According to her view of current affairs, she had three choices: One, she could pack up and go back to New York, reopen her job hunting files, and hope never to see Wolfe or Mc-Gavock again; two, she could stay on at McGavock Orchards until she was fired there too; three, she could drive down to New York this afternoon and fight for

101

her job and what was left of her relationship with Jonathan.

She covered her bowl of applesauce with aluminum foil and thought: *Jonathan McGavock* is *Ross Greening.*

Ha! So she'd been right about the apple connection! She shoved the bowl into the refrigerator.

To hell with Wolfe! She'd done her job, hadn't she? She'd found his damned elusive author. What did Wolfe expect? What did *McGavock* expect? He hadn't exactly been aboveboard with her either. He could have admitted who *he* was and—

And she couldn't forget him. There was no hope of that now. Probably there never had been once he'd fastened those gray-green eyes on her in the orchard office.

There was no doubt in her mind now. She knew what she had to do. She tossed some clothes into a suitcase, turned out the lights, locked the doors, and trotted downstairs to her Honda.

She would fight.

She stopped off at her apartment on West End Avenue to shower and change into a dark green wool challis dress. Since she had nothing but a minimum wage job picking apples, she took the crosstown bus to Wolfe's offices on East Fifty-eighth Street. She felt free and at home. Blissfully anonymous. She wondered if there were more people on the bus than in all of Rocky Springs. She hopped off at her stop and walked down to Wolfe's building. The air was clear and brisk, the streets alive, New York as wonderful to be in during autumn as New England. With every step Meg found herself gaining confidence. Jonathan McGavock/Ross Greening, in his ignominious jeans and flannel shirt, was on *her* turf now. Which just left Michael Wolfe. . . .

The lobby door was open, and the security guard remembered her, which only added to her self-confidence. She took the elevator up to the tenth floor and dug out her keys, just in case Wolfe chose not to let her in. *If* he and Jonathan were still around. She wasn't worried. If they weren't, she'd find them.

But the outer office door was unlocked, and when she pushed it open, she could hear their voices in Wolfe's office—Jonathan speaking in his languid baritone, Wolfe answering in his rapid-fire manner. She couldn't distinguish words, nor did she want to. Eavesdropping wasn't her style.

Without a second's hesitation she marched to Wolfe's door and announced herself with a single, decisive knock. Even as her employer demanded to know who had the nerve to disturb him, she pushed open the door and strode in.

"Oakes!" he yelled, none too pleased.

And Jonathan McGavock, aka Ross Greening, calmly leaned back in his leather chair and said, "Hello, there, Margaret T."

If she could have moved, she would have turned around and fled. So much for having Jonathan on her turf! He was smiling, so there were his dimples to contend with. He was looking at her, so there were his eyes to contend with. But, worst of all, he wasn't wearing disreputable jeans and a flannel shirt. Instead he was dressed in urban sartorial splendor: a gray-brown wool gabardine suit that fitted his broad shoulders and long legs so perfectly that it had to have been made for him.

He wasn't a burly woodsman stumbling around in the city. With a stiffening of her spine Meg realized that for the first time she was seeing the man who was Ross Greening. The best-selling novelist and, for the past weeks, her quarry.

Now she wondered who had been hunting whom.

It was Wolfe who snapped her back to her senses. "What the hell are you doing here, Oakes?" he demanded.

He was sitting on his massive leather chair behind his even more massive walnut desk. He did not have an impressive physique. He was under six feet, wiry, and white-haired, with a face that went with his name. But he was not unimpressive. He was always impeccably dressed and impeccably groomed, and he radiated power and intelligence. And, when he chose to, charm.

Obviously right now, Meg thought, he didn't choose to. "Excuse me," she said, feigning politeness, "but I assumed you two would be gone by now."

Wolfe gave a curt wave of his hand. "Out."

She smiled coolly. "If you don't mind, I'll go in and clean out my desk."

"That can wait until Monday, Oakes."

"No, it can't. I have to pick apples Monday morning." She glanced at Jonathan; his dimples were still showing. "At six A.M. on the dot."

Wolfe growled, but she ignored him and walked out, purposely leaving the door open behind her. "You don't leave with anything before I search you, Oakes!" he yelled.

One of the more unsavory names Wolfe was commonly called sprang to Meg's mind, but she stopped short of uttering it. She was determined to keep her cool. She walked through the reception area and went into the large office that held three desks. Hers was next to the window that looked out onto the street. "Lucky me," she muttered and sat down. Naturally she had no intention of clearing out her desk. She dug out a note pad and doodled. And waited.

Jonathan found her, not Wolfe. "Going to return the proposal from the woman in Tulsa?" he asked mildly, sitting on the edge of her desk.

"You knew?"

He smiled, unperturbed. "You should never have left me alone."

"You're a snake in the grass, Jonathan McGavock."

"Shall we slither out together?"

She wanted to laugh. He was so irreverent and self-controlled. But, of course he could afford to be. Why should her getting fired bother him? And the most Michael Wolfe could do to him was to tell the world his real name, but Wolfe wouldn't until he had exhausted his bag of tricks to get Ross Greening back into the fold—and even then he probably wouldn't. Hardhearted as he was, Wolfe did have a reputation to maintain among a long and impressive list of other authors. He wasn't one to cut off his nose to spite his face.

"Where's Wolfe?" she asked.

"In his office licking his wounds."

"I take it you weren't thrilled that he sent me after you?"

"He says he didn't send you," Jonathan informed

her matter-of-factly. "He claims you engineered the whole thing on your own—to impress him."

"*What?*"

"What better way to solidify your position at the Michael Wolfe Literary Agency than to wheel in their most successful former client?"

"He's making me his scapegoat!"

"The man's a shark, Meg."

She kicked back her chair and rose. "The man's a weasel. How dare he! I'm going in right now and—"

"Don't. He wants me back on his client roster, and if sacrificing you will do the trick, believe me, he'll do it. Let's work out an alternative plan."

"This is none of your affair. You've caused me enough trouble already. Why didn't you tell me you were on to me?"

He shrugged. "I wanted to see if you'd go so far as to actually pick apples."

"But—you mean you knew from the beginning?"

"More or less." His mouth twisted to one side in amusement. "Wolfe said you should have used an alias."

Meg stared in disbelief. "If you knew Wolfe sent me, why in the name of heaven did you hire me? If you'd just sent me packing like the other three orchards, I'd never have tracked you down!"

"Oh," he said, "that wouldn't have been as much fun."

"Fun! This isn't fun, McGavock. In case you haven't noticed, I am now without a job."

"There's always apple picking."

"Am I supposed to laugh?"

"Why not? It's better than crying."

"I don't cry, and I don't laugh."

He looked at her and laughed. "Then what do you do?"

She kicked her chair back under her desk and stalked toward the door. "I get even!"

"Where are you going?"

"If I had any sense, I'd go to Hartford and hire myself out to the first insurance firm that'd have me."

"Being a PR executive can't be as much fun as trying to outsmart a best-selling author and a high-powered literary agent."

"Will you stop with this fun business? I can't fight Wolfe."

"Then why did you come back to New York?"

"Wishful thinking," she said mournfully.

"And what about me?"

She eyed him for a moment. He looked stunning. Handsome and wealthy and successful and—just stunning. "I can't fight you either," she said quietly. "I don't even want to."

He smiled. "I was hoping you'd say that. Dinner?"

She smiled back. "I think I left evidence around my apartment that I'm really an apple picker from Connecticut."

He laughed a rich, deep, throaty laugh that made her breath catch. "Then why don't I take you to a restaurant?" he said and added with false self-mockery, "Why let these New York duds go to waste?"

"What about Wolfe?"

"With the mess I just laid on him, he'll be calling out for Chinese food into next week."

"I should talk to him—"

"You should leave him alone." Jonathan took her

arm and gave her an encouraging squeeze. "Trust me, Meg."

"I . . ." But his closeness, his confidence and promise squelched her doubts. "We've done so much to deserve each other's trust."

He grinned. "Haven't we, though?"

She laughed and slipped her hand into his, and together they left. There wasn't a sound coming from the office of the president of the Michael Wolfe Literary Agency.

CHAPTER SIX

Jonathan felt so right walking the streets of Manhattan with Meg at his side. Had he been a passerby, an unknown at a café table, this attractive and confident woman would have turned his head. Everything about her suggested that she thrived in a high-pressure job, belonged in Manhattan, loved her life there. Gone was the awkwardness he had seen when she had climbed his apple trees. He smiled to himself: gone, too, were the pink sneakers. Her dress was sophisticated and understated, and she moved with a stride that was long and determined and graceful. Her golden hair glistened in the sun, and her golden-flecked eyes danced in the shadows.

And yet the effects of her weeks in the country were there. He could see them in the healthy glow of her cheeks and the calluses forming on her hands, hear them in her laugh. They made her more real to him and connected her in a tangible way to a part of his world. Perhaps the best part.

Suddenly he wondered if calluses were forming on her heart as well, if, like her hands, it had been rubbed raw and was only beginning to protect itself with a thick, impenetrable shield. He should have followed his instincts and confronted her back in Rocky Springs with the announcement in *Publishers Weekly* or the proposal from Tulsa. But he'd taken a chance and acted on an impulse, and he'd cost Meg her job.

At least, he thought, for the time being. All he needed was a little more time. . . .

"You're awfully quiet," she said as they crossed Madison Avenue with a Saturday evening crowd.

He smiled. "It's the air pollution."

"On a day like today? Forget it. I think it's guilt."

He expected her to go on and explain, but she didn't. "Guilt?" he prompted.

"Uh-huh. For getting me fired."

"You got yourself fired."

"Ha! I was trying to spare a poor defenseless writer an unwanted confrontation with Michael Wolfe."

They stayed on East Fifty-sixth Street, and Jonathan glanced down at Meg, her stride unchanged. She didn't look at all stiff from her apple picking. Or upset about her job. She looked the way she had that day in the orchard office when she'd zapped him for his "platitude": irked but somehow unflappable. As if she knew getting turned down as an apple picker or getting fired from her job weren't the worst things that could happen to her. That somehow she would prevail.

"You were playing both sides against the middle, Ms. Oakes," he told her.

"I was *caught* in the middle."

"That implies a certain passivity, doesn't it? And I don't think you're passive, Margaret T. Not by a long shot. I think you weighed all the options, considered all the consequences, and made your decision."

She mumbled something that he didn't quite hear. Something, he thought, about dimples.

"I loathe Wolfe, you know."

"I like him." She looked up at him knowingly. "And I don't believe you. I think you like him too."

Jonathan managed not to smile. "He's an unethical, unscrupulous bastard."

"He claims the more bad names people think up to call him, the better an agent he must be. Makes his clients look like saints."

"His clients shouldn't be the ones thinking up the foul names."

Meg gave him a darting glance. "I don't think he'd care, as long as they remained his clients. Jonathan, Wolfe is ethical *and* scrupulous. He may cross lines you wouldn't cross, but his standards are well defined and inviolable. He lives and works by what he considers right. And his clients always come first."

"His own best interests always come first, Meg."

"And his best interests are his clients' best interests."

Jonathan was silent for a moment. "Not always."

"Unfortunately," she said with a resigned sigh, "they are rarely his associates' best interests."

"Yes," Jonathan agreed. "I wouldn't consider sending a green associate after a writer who told him two years ago to butt out of his life ethical or scrupulous, would you?"

"From his perspective, absolutely. He knows he has something to offer you. He wants to help."

Jonathan snorted. "He wants his damned commission!"

111

"What's wrong with that? What's best for you is best for him."

"Provided I—" He broke off in time; he didn't want to get into all that now, not in the middle of Manhattan with a temptingly impish woman at his side. "Not always."

She tugged on his sleeve. "And by the way, McGavock, I like to think of myself as peachy pink. Lizards are green."

"So are snakes," he said with a half-serious scowl, and Meg had the gall to laugh. Deliciously. Maybe Wolfe had known exactly what he was doing when he'd sent her after Ross Greening. "You're just like him, aren't you?"

"Trying," she said, unabashed.

"Are you serious?"

She laughed some more, and he still wondered if she was serious. He liked her unpredictability, her strength. She was a woman who wasn't waiting for a man to come along and protect her and shelter her from life. The right man for her would be one who wanted to build a life together with her, to share burdens and joys, to work out all the nitty-gritty details of day to day living, to grow with her and be with her. Meg, he thought, was a woman who took life by the horns and enjoyed what she could and endured what she had to. But it seemed to him that the bad times hadn't made her cynical, nor had they defeated her. She had not only survived but grown stronger. He liked that. He knew so little about her past, but he was positive beyond a single doubt that life hadn't always been easy for Meg. Hell, he thought, it wasn't easy now! She'd just been fired. But he wanted to know about her bad times, and her good times, and all the times in between.

As they walked along in silence it occurred to him that he wanted to know everything there was to know about Ms. Margaret T. Oakes. The prospect was appealing—very appealing indeed.

"When did you know I was Ross Greening?" he asked idly.

"Positively?" She shrugged, not worried that her answer would irritate him. "Not until my call to Wolfe this afternoon. My only reason for even being in Rocky Springs was to find you, of course, so naturally I was suspicious of everyone." She grinned: "Wolfe's training."

"I doubt it. He only had you for eight weeks."

"You're right, I suppose," she said, laughing. "He insisted I was part bloodhound to begin with, which is why he sent me to Connecticut instead of one of his other associates."

"And I would have recognized all his other associates," Jonathan put in dryly.

"Oh. Well, that too. Anyway, I looked everywhere for you, but Wolfe had tied my hands into so many knots, I could never really figure out a good game plan. Once I even managed to convince myself that Ross Greening was actually a woman and had hired a male model to fool Wolfe."

"What a devious mind you have, Margaret T.," Jonathan said. "Though I wish I'd thought of something like that."

"Oh, Wolfe still would have found you."

"Or his trusted associate. How did I end up on the top of your list of suspects?"

"Because of your 'impressive physique' and your orchards."

He stiffened some with surprise, but Meg was all business. Her tone was matter-of-fact, almost bland. "My orchards?"

"Greening *is* a variety of apple."

"Wolfe's idea?"

"Wolfe probably doesn't know apples grow on trees," she said, not at all vehemently, just stating the obvious. "It was my idea—and I considered it a long shot."

"That never occurred to me."

"You mean you didn't choose Ross Greening as your pseudonym because of greening apples?"

"I didn't own an orchard then," he told her. "So, no, I didn't."

She laughed. "I guess I'm even more clever than I thought—or not as."

"What about this impressive physique business? How did you know?" he asked with a touch of amusement.

"Wolfe," she said, obviously unaware of the subtle undertones of his banter. "He mentioned your scar, too, but that didn't do me any good. I mean, how was I supposed to get a look at your thighs?"

"Ask," he said. He was finding it difficult not to dwell on the alluring shape of her breasts and slender throat. "Men always like to show off their scars."

She shook her head, so preoccupied that she was taking him seriously. "No, then you would have been suspicious of *me.*"

He sighed. "But I already knew you worked for Wolfe."

"I didn't know you knew and—" She laughed unselfconsciously and cocked her head up at him. "Are you as confused as I am?"

"Only one thing doesn't make any sense to me."

"Why I wanted to pick your apples?"

He couldn't help it: he roared with laughter.

Meg was mortified. "I mean—*Jonathan!*"

"I'm sorry, Meg."

"You're not."

"True."

"Well? What are you confused about?"

He gave her an unrepentant leer but said honestly, "Why you're in such a good mood. You have a right to be furious with me, Meg, but instead we're going to have dinner together."

She shrugged. "Free food."

"Wolfe did say you were a sarcastic little chit," Jonathan muttered.

"When one is without gainful employment, one should watch one's pennies," she said with an innocent smile.

"What about picking my apples?"

She scowled up at him. "That is hardly gainful employment, and will you *stop?* I'll be purple with embarrassment by the time we get to the restaurant."

"Manuel would never approve."

"I'm sure."

"All right," he said as they turned up Fifth Avenue. "So you're having dinner with me because I'm paying. Presumably being in a good mood will get you to a better restaurant?"

"Fast food gives me indigestion." She added, her straight-faced look almost breaking into a grin, "Besides, you're a rich and famous writer. You can afford to take me out."

"Outspoken, aren't you?"

"I'll make a fabulous agent."

"Which brings me to the second half of my reason for confusion: Why aren't you furious with Wolfe too? He fired you, but you still defend him. You should at least be depressed."

"I'm not depressed because I've been in this position before. It's not so bad the second time, and getting depressed, unfortunately, does not get you employed. Otherwise I'd have never—Well, let's not get into that now. As for defending Wolfe: Why not?" She didn't give him a chance to start on his list of reasons. "Speaking of getting furious, I'm surprised you aren't out hanging me by my thumbs."

"You do cut right through all the niceties, don't you?"

"Eight weeks of working with Wolfe and one week of country living will do that to you."

"I suppose. Well, I'm not out hanging you by your thumbs because I'm not angry with you. Maybe I should be, but I'm not. It was only a matter of time before Wolfe hunted me down. I've known that all along. If I'd taken on another agent, he probably wouldn't have—"

"See: scruples."

"I guess," he agreed halfheartedly. "But I haven't shown my face in the publishing world in two years. That had to make Wolfe wonder."

"You provided him with a challenge."

"An excuse to come after me. Only the coward sent you instead."

116

"Imagine Wolfe applying at the orchard to pick apples," she said, already laughing.

Jonathan looked down at Meg and saw the glint in her eye. It was at once sensual and mischievous . . . and enticing. Suddenly he didn't care about Wolfe and Ross Greening and the past. He only cared about the future. A future with Meg. Looking at her now, he couldn't bring himself to picture Wolfe. And yet she continued to defend him. She *liked* him.

"He hates to leave New York, you know," she went on, her voice strangely breathless. "Can you imagine him climbing around in an apple tree?"

Jonathan had to laugh. "Art thought I was crazy enough as it was for hiring you, but Wolfe—no, I can't imagine him climbing around in an apple tree. I can't even imagine him sitting at one of the picnic tables eating an apple dumpling." He shook his head, smiling. "You two *are* different, aren't you?"

"To be sure," she said.

"Are you leering, Margaret T.?"

"Who, innocent me?"

"Innocent you, my foot!" He turned down a side street and stopped in front of a small, elegant Italian restaurant, his favorite in all of Manhattan. "Well, here we are. Shall we?"

Meg hesitated. "I should warn you: I had something to eat before I left town." She leaned toward him and whispered conspiratorially, "Hot dogs."

"Don't worry, love," he said easily, his eyes gleaming as much as hers. "I had a soft pretzel slathered with mustard for lunch. We won't tell Manuel. The poor man would have heart failure."

He opened the cream colored door with polished brass trim and held it, but Meg didn't go in at once.

"Don't you think we'll need reservations, Jonathan?" she asked.

She would ask, he thought dryly. "Yes, well—I've taken care of that."

She cocked her head, amused. "You mean you assumed I'd end up in New York?"

He bowed with mock chivalry. "I hoped, darling." He motioned for her to go in, then shut the door softly behind him and touched her shoulder, whispering in her ear, "And I should warn you: In New York I'm Ross Greening."

It was his only warning for what was to come.

The arrival of Manuel, the maître d', prevented Meg from asking Jonathan what he meant. Manuel greeted him warmly and called him Mr. Greening, and she understood. He was protecting his identity. It was as if he were two men, or wanted to be.

"Ah, and tonight you bring a beautiful woman," Manuel said with a strong Italian accent. "Welcome, welcome. We have your room ready, of course."

His *room?* Meg wondered.

Jonathan, however, didn't look the least bit surprised or ill at ease. In fact, she thought, he looked as confident and strong and at home as he had wielding his monstrous ax. He belonged here in an elegant midtown restaurant as much as he belonged in a Connecticut apple orchard.

Manuel led them past the bar and up a narrow staircase to a small but exquisitely decorated private dining room. The table was covered with white linen, a crystal vase of yellow roses in the center, and set elaborately for two. Manuel introduced them to their waiter and left silently.

Meg quirked an eyebrow. "Well, well."

"One of the benefits of a vivid imagination," Jonathan said, amused.

Jonathan requested scotch, not naming the brand because the waiter already knew, and after a second's hesitation Meg requested the same.

She rolled her tongue along the inside of her cheek. "No cat in the middle of the table?"

Jonathan laughed. "Not without a white sauce, anyway."

"Yuck."

"That's what you get for being impertinent."

"You're a cruel man," she said, grinning. "This *is* a tad different from your farmhouse, you have to admit."

"Of course. That's where Jonathan McGavock lives." His gray-green eyes gleamed. "He wouldn't be comfortable here."

"You're not amusing, *Ross.* You are Jonathan McGavock. And he's you."

He smiled wryly. "So Wolfe keeps telling me."

"He's right," she said emphatically.

"Good ol' feet-flat-on-the-floor Margaret T."

"As Wolfe says, our job is to stay on Mother Earth so all you creative types can do your thing without getting into trouble. *We* don't have vivid imaginations."

"I can't imagine why Wolfe fired you. You're cut from the same cloth."

"He also says ninety percent of an agent's job is

licking clients' wounds, five percent is licking stamps, and the other five percent is—"

"Meg," he warned.

She grinned ingenuously and finished, "negotiating contracts."

"There you go defending him again."

"Quoting."

"He fired you, damn it!"

"Oh, pooh. I don't pay any attention to what employers do and say on weekends."

"Then you don't think he meant it?"

"Do you?"

"I've never been able to second-guess Wolfe."

"Ta-da. Then he's the perfect agent for you. Why have an agent you can second-guess? You might as well do everything on your own."

Jonathan shook his head. "You're impossible. I assume you want to go on working for him?"

"Sure." She grinned. "I like licking clients' wounds."

"Lady," he said dangerously, "you're going to get yourself in a heap of trouble."

She laughed, unintimidated. "And here I thought I already was in a heap of trouble." The waiter returned with their drinks. Meg tried the scotch. "Very smooth."

"It damned well ought to be," Jonathan muttered.

"My, my, that sounded like a surly woodsman I know from Connecticut."

"The oaf who chops his own wood?"

"The very same." She tried another sip of her scotch. "This is nice. Do you come here often?"

"It depends. I used to come here frequently with

friends—New York friends, mostly. People who know me only as Ross Greening. During the last two years I haven't seen those friends much though. Consequently my evenings here have been infrequent and solitary." He smiled and added quietly, "Until tonight."

Meg looked thoughtful. "Doesn't anyone know you as both Jonathan McGavock and Ross Greening?"

"Michael Wolfe. You. My banker and lawyer." He smiled. "My mother and sister."

"What about friends?"

"No."

"Does that mean I'm not a friend?"

"Darling, you're in a category all by yourself." He smiled tenderly, the corners of his eyes crinkling, softening his look. "And I'm glad you're here."

The waiter appeared then, and he and Ross/Jonathan quietly discussed the menu and timing. Meg sat back, enjoying herself, marveling at Jonathan's easy sophistication. She tried to picture him wielding his ax, and found that she could. He was a complicated man, talented and yet down to earth, uncompromisingly masculine and yet beautifully sensitive. In spite of his two names and two identities he was after all only one man. Meg was intrigued but, she thought, not at all confused.

Meg couldn't remember when she had eaten a more exquisite dinner. Each course was designed to complement what preceded it and what followed it. Everything was carefully chosen and perfectly cooked. She found herself unable and unwilling to engage in serious conversation. It was an evening that aroused all of her senses and precluded thoughts of reclusive writers and high-powered agents. Meg became intensely aware of tastes and textures, of sights and sounds . . . and, most of all, of the man seated across from her. He spoke of evenings spent in that same room with literary friends, of exotic meals, of the occasion during the height of his fame when a reporter bribed a waiter and hid behind the small private bar in the hope of learning more about the real Ross Greening.

"I was the one who found him," Jonathan explained.

"Poor man," Meg said with feeling.

"I can always smell a snoop."

"So I've discovered."

"I confiscated the film in his camera—although he hadn't had a chance to use it—and escorted him outside."

"Manuel must have paled."

Jonathan grinned. "It took three of us to revive him."

"Did the reporter sue you?"

"He didn't dare."

"And obviously he didn't learn your true identity."

"How could he? No one there that night knew my true identity. They would have recognized me if they had walked into the barn at the orchards, of course, but first they would have had to know where to look."

"And what happened to the waiter?"

"Summarily fired."

Meg smiled thoughtfully. "I'll add that story to my list of things Wolfe should have told me but never did."

It was the closest they had come to serious conversation, but a fresh bottle of wine arrived, and they both tasted it and went on to a new subject. Meg was being mesmerized by Jonathan. He was the same man she had known in Rocky Springs: infuriating, endearing, seductive, astute. But she was seeing another dimension of him. Not another Jonathan, but a part of him that somehow didn't fit into his rustic life in Connecticut. It just wasn't needed there.

After dinner they went out onto the street and walked over to Fifth Avenue. "The night air's warmer here than in the country," Meg pointed out.

"All the concrete keeps it from cooling off so quickly," he said. "Care to walk?"

"Just walk, or walk someplace?"

"I have an apartment about ten blocks from here."

She smiled. "Naturally."

"I can't surprise you anymore, can I?"

"Oh, I'm sure you could."

"What if I told you I'm really just an apple grower and forester and not Ross Greening at all?"

"I wouldn't believe you," she said, feeling very warm when his hand slipped into hers, "not after tonight."

"Are you implying foresters don't know enough to take a woman to dinner in New York?"

"Not at all. I'm just saying you're *not* just Jonathan McGavock of New Rocky Springs. Your stories were too convincing, *Ross.* And it's not what you do, it's who you are. You're a writer, a forester, an apple grower—you're just you, damn it."

He laughed softly, taking his hand from hers and easing it around her waist. "Darling, you don't have to convince me. I already know."

"Then why the reclusive act?"

"Later, Meg."

"How later?"

His eyes sparkled. "Later tonight?"

"Meaning?"

"Meaning I want you to come back to my apartment with me."

"Your apartment," she said, feeling the warmth of his touch and his promise coursing up her back, "or Ross Greening's?"

He grinned, amused. "It's in my name—for the sake of privacy."

"Then your landlord knows who you are."

"No. He only cares that I can afford my rent."

"And, of course, you can."

"Ross Greening can," he said with a light pat on her waist.

"You're maddening."

"I've never had the opportunity to be two men with one woman," he said lightly. "I'm enjoying myself."

She noticed the spring in his step. "You're not two men," she said.

"So you say, but you didn't expect your woodsman from Rocky Springs to be wearing a suit, did you?" His smile flashed in the darkness. "Especially one that fit."

Meg, however, was still not buying. "*You* didn't expect an urban type like me to wear pink sneakers and jeans to pick apples."

"They just aren't you, Meg," he said with mock seriousness.

"Sure they are—because *I'm* me."

He glanced down at her. "Without a doubt, my love, without a doubt. I can see you're not going to indulge my schizophrenia."

She couldn't stop a grin. "I'm not going to indulge your warped sense of humor!"

He sighed, still not serious. "And I so wanted to try again."

Meg was confused. "Try what again?"

"Making you laugh—and maybe tucking you in." His gait, she thought, was positively jaunty. "I wanted to try again. We were still playing guessing games with each other last night, remember?"

"I remember. And you had the last word."

"I always do. That's something to keep in mind about me, love."

"I'm learning, Jonathan, I'm learning." She swung out of his arm and leaped in front of him, so that he nearly toppled into her. He stopped just in time, steadying himself by grabbing her shoulders. "Good reflexes," she said, wryly amused. "That's the forester in you."

"Meg—"

"Ooh, there's a dangerous look in the man's eye. I thought you were Ross Greening in New York?"

His hands slid down to her waist and stayed. "What do you think you're doing, Margaret Oakes?"

"I'm trying to figure out who I'm going to be with for the next . . . whatever."

"You'll be with me."

"Ross Greening or Jonathan McGavock?"

"Both," he said, "and neither. Just me."

She laughed and swung back to his side. "Sounds fascinating."

"It will be," he promised, "it will be."

CHAPTER SEVEN

Jonathan stopped at an unprepossessing gray-stone building and announced, "This is it."

Meg did not mention that even her humble building on the West Side had a more attractive front door. His was security-minded but downright ugly. The inside entry smelled of new indoor-outdoor carpeting. Tweedy-looking, of course. The row of mailboxes were of the same functional type as those in Meg's building: skinny silver boxes with a hodgepodge of things stuck to them to identify to whom they belonged; a vertical row of yellowed buttons, apartment number and name beside each, to the right of the boxes. Pasted next to the 6–E button and stuck on the 6–E mailbox was *McGavock*. Even without the apple logo Meg immediately recognized the type from the McGavock Orchards stationery.

"Six–E?" she said. "Does that mean sixth floor?"

Jonathan was unlocking the inside door, equally as ugly as the outer door. Meg knew that, once upon a tasteful time, the building had been graced with a beautiful door of oak or walnut, or maybe even mahogany.

"And you call yourself a New Yorker," Jonathan said as he pushed open the door.

She saw at once it was a walk-up. "We might as well have gone to my place," she grumbled.

"What were you expecting, Margaret T.?" he asked cheerily.

"An elevator," she replied.

He laughed. "My private dining room misled you."

They walked up the six flights of stairs. Neither was puffing when they reached apartment 6–E. "See what a little apple picking will do for you?" Jonathan said.

"Don't take credit, McGavock," she warned with a gleam in her eye. "*I* live on the fifth floor of a walk-up. I do this every day."

"It's good exercise," he pronounced and opened the door.

Meg had warned herself not to expect anything of Ross Greening/Jonathan McGavock, but, nevertheless, when she walked into the apartment, she knew it wasn't quite what she had anticipated.

"Let me give you the grand tour," Jonathan offered happily. "It'll take about ten seconds."

He grabbed her hand, and she trailed after him. The rooms—a living room, dining area, kitchen, bathroom, and two bedrooms, one of which she didn't see—were small. Except for the dutiful exposed brick wall, all the walls were painted in neutral colors rather than papered. The furnishings were expensive, but not outlandishly so, and tasteful, but not noticeably so. There was no hint of a New York decorator's hand. The bathroom had a pedestal sink and a tub with legs. The kitchen was too small, but every inch of corner, crevice, and wall was put to use. There was no dust or clutter, which Meg thought peculiar.

"Well, what do you think?" he asked in a tone that implied he already knew.

"It reminds me of my place on West End Avenue," she said, sitting on the dark brown corduroy love seat. "Except I have only one bedroom, and your stove's bigger."

"I eat more," he said.

"And have more guests?"

"No, I just need room to spread out."

"Ahh," she said, although she hadn't the slightest idea why.

He sat beside her. "Disappointed?"

"I was hoping for a penthouse view of Manhattan."

"Is that the kind of place Ross Greening would have?"

She grinned up at him, conscious now of how close he was. "Indubitably."

"What about Jonathan McGavock?"

"He would have a couple of rooms in some rathole of a building and would use them only when he was in town for a Yankee game, and then under protest, preferring, of course, to drive back to Connecticut that same night."

"Yankees? He's a die-hard Red Sox fan."

"So he'd come to Yankee Stadium and cheer the Red Sox and start a brawl," she replied, undaunted.

Jonathan grunted. "You are a sarcastic little snip, aren't you?"

"Chit," she corrected sarcastically.

"No wonder you ended up working for Wolfe. He's not intimidated by you, is he?"

"Wolfe isn't intimidated by anything."

"True, but it helps to have a boss who'll let you be yourself."

She sighed. "That's what I thought."

"Depressed?"

"Determined." She smiled and pushed aside a thought about his mouth. "Why no penthouse?"

"If you were a well-known writer who prefers to shun publicity and jealously guards his privacy, would you install yourself in a New York penthouse?"

She shook her head. "Probably not. Too flashy."

"Exactly. My landlord knows me as a successful forest management consultant who has a comfortable but not too noticeable apartment in New York." Jonathan settled back against the couch and lifted his feet onto the sturdy coffee table. When he leaned back, his thighs brushed Meg's hip. "Besides," he went on, satisfied, "I like it here."

Meg kicked off her shoes and tucked her feet up under her. With her knees bent they touched Jonathan's thighs. He didn't seem to mind the contact, so she didn't move back. "I hate to bring this up," she said, "but does Wolfe know about this place?"

"Are you kidding? Of course not. He'd have put a twenty-four-hour guard on the building and monitored all my moves."

"For two years?"

"For a decade, if necessary. He'd have waited for his chance and then pounced."

Meg looked dubious. "He could have done that in Rocky Springs."

"He *did* do it in Rocky Springs—he simply used an intermediary."

"Me."

"He knew he'd never get close to me."

"He had your post office box number and knew your real name," Meg pointed out. "All he had to do was show up in town and ask around."

"So why didn't he?"

She thought. "You'd have found out he was in town before he could track you down."

"You got it."

"He also wanted a third party's opinion of you. He wanted to know what he was getting into—*if* he should get into anything. Jonathan, I honestly believe Wolfe would have left you alone if I recommended it. I —" She broke off. "Let's not talk about Wolfe."

"Just one thing," Jonathan said seriously. "Are you going to give him this address?"

"Why should I?"

"To get your job back."

"It wouldn't work," she snapped. "He's already found you, remember?"

"Yes, so he has—for now."

"What's that supposed to mean?"

"Nothing." He smiled, touching her hair. "You're right. Let's not talk about Wolfe. Or writing or jobs— or anything."

"Jonathan . . ."

He was staring, holding her with his eyes, so that she couldn't move and didn't want to speak. There was nothing angry in his stare, nothing threatening, and still she felt her breath catch.

"You're beautiful, Meg."

The simple words softened the intensity of his look, helped to explain it. Meg felt as if she were sitting

130

there beside him wearing nothing at all, because she knew that was how he saw her.

"I don't know what to say," she said honestly.

He smiled, moving his hand down along her throat. "Is that a first?"

"I'm a woman of few words."

He was laughing when his hand reached her breasts, but the warmth of his touch, which she could feel even through her clothing, stifled her response. His laughter died quickly, suddenly, and his eyes locked with hers.

"I want to spend the night with you," he said, his voice husky and deep but very sure. "Stay here with me, Meg. Let me love you."

She reached out, not at all tentatively, and with two fingers lifted a lock of auburn-tinted hair that had fallen across his forehead. "And can I love you, Jonathan McGavock?"

"Till you can't stand it anymore, sweetheart."

His mouth covered hers, catching her smile, and her hand slipped down his back. He felt so strong. So hard and impenetrable. When his tongue gently entered her mouth, she thought: and sensitive, too.

And then she could feel his stiffening—his back, his tongue, his arms—and all distance from what was happening between them disappeared. All thought vanished. She could sense his urgency, feel it burning against her, and all at once it was inside her, burning within her, stiffening her limbs. She responded fully and openly to his kiss, making it theirs, pressing her body against his, silently asking for more of him, silently offering more of herself.

131

He moaned softly into her mouth. "I know there's so much we haven't discussed. . . ."

"It can wait," she said, a desperation creeping into her tone, one that reassured rather than frightened her. She could feel; she could love; the day was not lost. "Please, Jonathan, let it wait."

"Gladly." He laughed and swept her into his arms.

He pulled back the goosedown comforter and laid her on the sheets. Even through her dress, she could feel their coolness against her overheated body. Her eyes never left his as he remained standing and pulled off his tie. His jacket followed, and he started on his shirt. She watched, hypnotized by his sure movements, his strength. He dropped the shirt onto a chair and tugged off the undershirt. His chest was magnificent: broad, dark, taut, utterly masculine. Her fingertips wriggled with the urge to wander through the thick, black hairs.

She sat up and reached behind her for the buttons to her challis dress. Her fingers were tensed, trembling with a thrilling passion, and the simple task became one of increasing frustration. Jonathan smiled and dropped onto his knees next to her. "Here, let me," he said.

But his movements were just as awkward, and soon he was frustrated too. "Damned things," he muttered. "I ought to just tear this off you—"

"Don't!" she protested, laughing. "I didn't bring a change of clothes. You want me to get arrested on my way home tomorrow?"

"How come I managed an entire shirt full of buttons, and I can't undo three little pearly buttons—

Wait, here we go. One, two, three. I trust everything else will come with ease?"

She grinned. "I'll let you know."

"How 'bout I find out for myself?" he suggested, grinning back.

"Fine with me."

He shoved her gently down onto the bed and lifted the dress over her head. She lay limp, like a rag doll, letting him do as he would. He had to lift her arms and put them back down at her side, but he did so effortlessly. She started to shiver at the cool sheets touching her skin.

"Want me to turn up the heat?" he asked.

"I don't think that'll be necessary."

"You're shivering."

"Kiss me."

He did, lingeringly, as he unfastened the front clasp of her bra. He didn't stumble once.

"There," she breathed, the taste of his tongue still in her mouth. "Better."

"Good," he murmured, landing tiny kisses along her throat, deeper, until he captured a pointed nipple between his lips. "Does this help?"

"Jonathan . . . I'll be burning up soon."

"That's the whole idea, love."

He kissed a searing trail down her smooth, firm abdomen, until he reached the waist of her underpants and panty hose. He rose up, straddling her with his knees planted firmly on either side of her hips, and slowly, achingly, drew down those final garments. She was beautifully, agonizingly aware of every point of contact between his hands and her skin. With a swift, agile movement he dropped down off the bed, swept off her underpants and panty hose, and paused to gently rub her knees.

"You're beautiful, Meg . . . beautiful . . ."

Even if she could have answered, she wouldn't have known what to say. But her body was bursting with longing, burning with the throbbing heat of desire, and she knew speech was impossible.

Then he was kissing her knees, teasing and tickling and tempting with tiny, feathery caresses that were incredibly erotic. His mouth moved upward, along her thighs, his lips and tongue and teeth all coordinating to drive her to a point of ecstasy she had never before experienced.

She was hardly aware when he moved away and pulled off his pants, casting them atop the jumble of clothes. He came to her again, quickly, and even as she reveled in the feel of his long, naked, hard body against hers, she sensed that speech was just as impossible for him. There would be no words of love, at least not for now. She didn't mind. They were, she thought, suddenly unnecessary.

Their eyes locked for an instant, and then with one swift thrust, he entered her, and Meg felt as if he'd joined them in a precious union, thrown them both into a fire of their own making. They put the fire out together—slowly, wondrously, thoroughly. There was no need, Meg thought, to leave any coals burning for later. They could build a fire of their own anytime, anywhere, ignite it with a kiss, extinguish it with their passion. She smiled happily, dreamily as she settled into his arms and felt his heart pumping next to her cheek.

"Darling Meg," he said, and they drifted off to sleep together.

Dawn was slanting in through Jonathan's barred windows when Meg bolted straight up in bed and yelled, *"The scar!"*

Beside her the goosedown comforter flew back, and a large browned body snapped up beside her. "Where?" Jonathan bellowed, instantly alert. "Damn it, no one's broken into this apartment in five years! Wait here while I check it out." He shoved the comforter over her head.

"Jonathan." Meg pulled the comforter down, her hair going every which away. "Calm down. There is no burglar."

He glared at her. His hair was tousled, but his eyes were alert. "But I heard you yell," he stated darkly.

"Yes, well, not because of a burglar."

"Margaret . . ."

"I remembered your scar."

"My scar?" He stared, not certain he had heard correctly. Then understanding dawned, and he roared, *"My scar!"*

"The eighty-stitch scar from your chain saw accident," she explained needlessly. "I forgot to look last night."

"You woke me up so you could see my scar!"

"No," she countered, calm. "I remembered your scar, and I yelled. I was talking to myself."

"You were talking rather loudly, m'dear."

"I didn't mean to wake you."

"Meg, it's six o'clock in the morning."

"Is it that late?" She glanced around at the digital clock: 5:57. He hadn't exaggerated.

"We were up till all hours, remember?"

His shoulders seemed closer, more massive in the confines of the small bedroom. With a quickening of her heartbeat she remembered. She had the comforter held over her breasts, not ill at ease, but not entirely comfortable either. She felt . . . different.

"You're used to getting up early," she pointed out.

"I am?"

"To pick—no, you don't do the picking, do you?" she corrected herself. "You're a woodsman," she declared, as if that explained whatever needed to be explained and excused everything else.

Jonathan called her bluff. "So?"

"So there must be many a cold and damp morning when you have to get up to go saw wood . . . or whatever."

He was almost laughing. "Margaret," he said, "this is New York."

"Old habits die hard."

"I haven't gotten up this early since—I don't know, it's been weeks."

"I know people who have never seen six A.M."

"Mention that man's name, and you're in worse trouble."

"Worse trouble? I'm not in any trouble. Look at you, you're wide awake and chipper. We could go jogging through Central Park. Think of it. The two of us in our sweat pants—"

"You only have that dress of yours."

"I could borrow your sweat pants."

"They'd never fit."

She sighed. "You've ruined me, Jonathan."

He grinned lecherously. "Have I, now?"

She ignored his comment, pretended she hadn't reacted, that her heart was beating normally and her skin was cool and her mind was steady. "McGavock Orchards, I mean," she said, as if catching herself. "Apple picking at dawn. Getting up with the crows. Do you suppose there are any crows in New York?"

"Meg, you're up too early," he said, feeling her forehead. "See? A temperature. You need your rest."

"I'm not tired."

"I am."

"Well, you can go back to sleep—after you've shown me your scar, of course." She gave him the most earnest businesslike look she could under the circumstances. It would have been worse, she thought, if she didn't have a corner of the comforter. "To think," she went on airily, "I could have slept with an impostor."

"And what's *that* supposed to mean?"

"Maybe you're not Ross Greening."

"And so what if I'm not? Wasn't sleeping with Jonathan McGavock good enough?"

"Uh-oh."

He grinned. "Trapped."

"Cornered."

"Bound and gagged."

"I don't get to see your scar?"

His grin broadened. "That all depends, m'love."

"On?"

"On whether you know where to look—and how."

"And when?"

"Now will do."

137

She dropped the comforter and dove, but he caught her by the shoulders and shoved her back down on the bed. They both were laughing. His mouth found hers, and they kissed hungrily, Meg feeling bolder than she had the night before, more alert and confident. She plundered his mouth with all the daring and vigor with which he plundered hers. A welcome ache welled up inside her.

Jonathan's hand slipped beneath the covers and caught her around the thigh. His fingers caressed the sensitive skin of her inner thigh. "It's right about here," he murmured.

"Yes," she breathed, "I can feel it, Jonathan. . . ."

He laughed softly. "My scar," he said, "the one on my leg—remember?"

"Oh. *Oh!* Of course I remember! I—"

And her hand shot under the covers and stabbed blindly downward, but it caught something besides his thigh. Jonathan was smiling. "Please," he said, "go on."

"I don't know if I can."

"Then allow me."

He leaned toward her, pressing himself more firmly into her hand, and his mouth covered hers. His tongue caressed her lips with a liquid warmth that flowed down through her body. She moaned, letting her other hand trail lightly up his arm until her fingers slid into the thickness of his hair.

"I'd wake up at six every morning for this," he murmured, kissing her chin, her throat, and then, at his own pace, taking a straining nipple into his mouth.

She cried out with pleasure and want, and he moved onto her, straddling her, so that she could take him by

138

his lean, hard hips and urge him downward and into her. He held himself aloft, though, until he had taken the other nipple into his mouth and fired it with his liquid warmth and she had cried out again, more loudly this time. And then he moaned, and she clenched his hips with a desperation born of passion. He thrust into her, a hard, sure, clean thrust that brought a groan of pure and unabashed ecstasy to her lips.

For a long, long time they were one, moving, breathing, thinking, acting as a unit, loving and being loved, satisfying and being satisfied. Meg lost all sense of time and place. She could have been anywhere—on a beach, in a field, in her apartment. It wouldn't have mattered, as long as Jonathan was with her. Nothing mattered, as long as he was with her. She could meet any challenge, do anything and be anything, but she needed him in her life. Life without him was unimaginable.

When the climax came, and she cried out with the thrill of his body in hers, she collapsed against him. They were both spent and exhausted, breathing as hard as they would have had they gone out jogging in Central Park. Meg kissed his shoulder and tasted the salt of his perspiration. She smiled and laughed. "I can't move," she said.

"Then don't," he murmured, securing his arm around her waist and kissing the top of her head. "We're not going anywhere."

"Jonathan—" She broke off, too overwhelmed and satisfied and tired to clarify her thoughts. She was so damned happy! And she wanted him to know, but the words just weren't going to come. "Jonathan, I'm glad I met you."

He laughed and hugged her close. "And I'm glad I met you, Margaret T.—very glad."

She fell asleep in his arms, having quite forgotten the scar.

She saw the scar when they were getting dressed. It was a clean reddish ridge that ran on a slant along his inner thigh. "It's not that disgusting," Meg pronounced. "I expected a chain saw would make a more ragged wound."

"It did," Jonathan said dryly, pulling up his jeans.

Meg ran her fingers through her damp hair. A shower had revived her, but Jonathan had greeted her when she stepped out. One thing had led to another, and soon they were making love right there on the bath mat. She had required a second shower. "What happened?" she asked curiously.

"You really don't want to know the details, Meg."

"Sure I do. I have a strong stomach."

"I was limbing a tree with a friend of mine—"

"Oh, my God, no more! How awful."

He gave her a sour look. "You're not terribly funny, you know."

She grinned. "Cute?"

"Adorable," he said, unable to stop a smile.

"Go on." She crossed her heart. "Not another word, I promise. You were limbing a tree with a friend."

"Technically it should be a one-man job. It's safer that way, but we were in a rush, so we were working on it together."

Meg shook her head solemnly, pulling on her panty hose. "Not very bright."

"Your mouth is going to get you into trouble, toots."

"It has before."

"Not with me—yet," he said dangerously.

She smiled. "I was supposed to keep quiet, wasn't I?" She grabbed her dress off the floor and shook out the wrinkles. "Thank heavens for challis," she muttered and smiled innocently up at Jonathan, glaring at her as he buttoned his chamois shirt. "Go on."

"I was also using a chain saw that was actually too big for the job—and *don't* say a word, or you'll find your behind out the door."

"Better than over your knee, I suppose," she said, unable to resist some sort of comment.

"Don't tempt me. At any rate, while I was working on one branch, Bosco was down a few yards—"

"Bosco?"

"Yes," he said darkly, "Bosco. Stanley Boscovitch."

"Bosco," she repeated, tongue in cheek. "Stan would be too simple, wouldn't it?"

"He's not a Stan. He's a Bosco—and a friend."

"In Connecticut?"

"Montana. I was there for a few weeks trying to forget I was Ross Greening. Do you want me to continue, or have you heard enough?"

She waved a hand just as she pulled her dress over her head. "No, no, go on," she said through the challis. "I can't imagine what happens next."

"Bosco and I were cutting off limbs simultaneously. He finished his first, the tree turned slightly, and instead of sawing on an oak limb, I was sawing on—"

141

"Oh, *yuck!*"

She smoothed out her dress and reached behind her to fasten the buttons. Jonathan watched with a smug smile. "Would you like me to describe how the saw jumped when it hit and—"

"I get the idea, McGavock."

He laughed. "All right, I'll spare you, but you're missing the best part. The wound was not neat, to say the least, and I ruined a perfectly good pair of pants."

"What about the chain saw?"

"I threw it as hard as I damned well could, but didn't do it a lick of damage."

"How did you end up with such a neat scar?"

"The doctor I went to was finicky—and had sewed up this kind of wound before." Jonathan paused and added dryly, remembering, "He was not sympathetic. Actually, though, I was lucky. I came out of it with no major muscle or nerve damage."

Meg couldn't suppress a shudder. "And you still use a chain saw?"

"Sure. I was back in the woods within a few weeks." He grinned at Meg's pale face. "Sweetheart, it's a mistake you only make once, and all things considered, I was very lucky. I know a man who—"

"Enough!"

He laughed. "All right. I only got as far as describing the chain saw before Wolfe stopped me. I think he was disappointed I wasn't laid up longer so I could write more."

Meg slipped on her shoes. "Then you were still writing when the accident happened?"

"Like a maniac, my love, like a maniac."

She opened her mouth for another question, but

Jonathan smiled, showing his dimples, and suggested a small, quiet restaurant where they could get a light brunch. "No private dining room, though," he said with feigned disappointment. "We'll have to eat with the peons."

Meg laughed. "Just my type."

Jonathan took her hand, his eyes shining. "Mine too."

CHAPTER EIGHT

After a quiet and delightful champagne brunch on the East Side, Jonathan drove Meg to her apartment. He expected something affordable, but with a hint of "upscale" and businesslike sophistication. An electric coffee grinder and museum-mounted prints, that sort of thing.

What he found was clutter. Papers, files, books, magazines, even junk mail were stacked wherever there was space: on the love seat, the Windsor chairs, the small Queen Anne table, the built-in shelves flanking the fireplace, the floor. He did have to admit, however, that the piles were neat. And somehow the little apartment, with its pale gray-blue walls and worn Persian carpet and cross-stitched sampler and all its clutter, was Meg. Just Meg. This was where she came to be herself, and it reflected all that she was.

He stepped over a stack of used mailbags, their original address labels torn off. "Waste not, want not," he commented. "Who called whom a cheap Yankee?"

"I'm not a Yankee," she said, hovering behind him with her hands wrung together.

He laughed. "You'll do."

"My place is a little messy right now," she explained, not apologizing. "I don't have an office, so it's hard to organize my space. Just a cubbyhole somewhere would make all the difference in the world."

He looked around at her. "So would a wrecking crane."

"I know where everything is," she maintained.

"Shall I quiz you?" he asked, ambling past the Queen Anne table. At least he *thought* it was Queen Anne. He couldn't be sure. Piled on top of it were several dozen query letters, each paper-clipped with its own stamped, self-addressed envelope. Piled beneath it, concealing the telltale legs, were several dozen paperback novels and the most ragged Webster's dictionary he'd ever seen. "You can't possibly remember what you have in here, never mind know where it is."

"You're not being very chivalrous," she pointed out.

"I'm not the chivalrous type," he said matter-of-factly as he noted that the living room and dining area overlooked the street. He also noted the dead spider plant in the window. Jonathan thought about it for a moment, but he was quite sure he'd never been quite so charmed by a deceased plant. "Comes from all those years of living in the woods," he went on. "There weren't all that many people around—certainly not the type that would appreciate chivalry—and it's difficult to play Sir Lancelot to creatures that steal your food."

"I'm not a creature, and I would never steal your food."

"But you're not the type that would appreciate chivalry," he taunted. "Admit it, love: You like me crass and brutally honest."

145

She laughed. "I adore you, but I don't think you're as crass and brutally honest as you think you are."

"Want me to improve my record?"

"No!" She gestured broadly at the mess surrounding them. "It's not always this bad. I went straight from job hunting to working for Wolfe to hunting for you to . . . to I don't know what. Anyway, I'm not organized yet. I haven't even found a place to put the stuff from my *last* job. Though most of this is from the agency. But Wolfe told me to put everything on hold until we took care of you."

"Sounds ominous," Jonathan said, turning away from the windows. "What about Tulsa?"

"Oh, I brought a few proposals I thought might be promising along with me for quiet evenings. Wolfe wouldn't have approved, of course, but I honestly never expected to find you. You told him you peeked under my couch cushion, I suppose?"

He bowed. "Naturally."

"Cad."

"Darling," he said with a rakish look, "when you jump into the ring with me, you'd better be prepared to fight."

"Oh, I was prepared to fight," she said, sitting on top of a pile of manuscripts on the Windsor chair next to her telephone answering machine. "I just wasn't prepared to lose."

"You never are, are you?"

She fiddled with the tape recorder. "I'm learning."

"Meg, what the hell are you doing?"

"Checking my messages. I put the machine on yesterday when I stopped by to change."

Jonathan shook his head. "Compulsive, aren't you?"

"Just thorough—and you can see where it's gotten me."

She played back the tape and found she had had one caller: the president of the Michael Wolfe Literary Agency. His message was short and to the point: "Oakes? My office, ten A.M., Monday. I want a full report, including where the hell you are right now."

Furious, Meg banged the machine off. Jonathan sat back and laughed. "How did I ever end up working for that man?" she said in disgust. "I don't believe him!"

"You ended up working for him because your minds operate on the same wavelength, and you do believe him," Jonathan said laconically. "You said yourself you wouldn't consider yourself fired until Monday."

She crossed her arms in a huff. "I am not going to kowtow to Michael Wolfe."

"No, but you will do your job. He knows you will, Meg." Jonathan smiled tenderly. "And so do I."

"He made me his scapegoat!"

"That's what associates are for."

Still seething, she leaped up and dumped a stack of files on the floor to free up an antique pine rocking chair. Then she plopped down. "The man's an insensitive brute."

Jonathan stretched out his legs, crossing his ankles, and regarded Meg with some amusement. He appreciated her dilemma, but not for a moment did he buy her anger. Her golden eyes were sparkling, her cheeks flushed with excitement. "You're glad he called, Meg," he suggested quietly. "He's giving you the opening you

147

need to keep your job. You're a fighter, darling." *And so am I,* he thought.

"I can't go on working for Wolfe, Jonathan, not if it means—" She broke off and shook her head, the sparkle gone from her eyes. "I won't do it. There are battles you just can't win no matter what you do. This is one of them."

Jonathan said nothing. This was the tricky part, he thought; the critical moment. He'd anticipated it when he'd arrived in New York yesterday afternoon. But that didn't make knowing what to do any easier.

"Meg, you and Wolfe make a damned impressive team," he said at length. "After a few months together you'll have half the publishers in New York eating out of your hands and the other half intimidated as hell. You're too outspoken for public relations, but you're a born agent, Margaret T."

She looked away, but before she did, he saw the tears glistening in her eyes. "You don't understand, Jonathan."

"I'm not naïve," he said gravely. "I do understand."

"I can't lie to him. I can't pretend you're just another client. He won't care whether we slept together, Jonathan, but he'll ask where we went. And I'll have to tell him. You understand that, don't you? Your apartment, your private dining room—*he'll know.* And that's only the beginning. He'll want to know every detail about your life in Rocky Springs—what your house looks like, what kind of cars you drive, what kind of people you hire, what your orchards are like. He'll even want to know about the damned cat that sleeps in the middle of your kitchen table! And do you want to know why?"

"Because he wants to know if I have another book in me—if he doesn't have his answer already."

"That's my point exactly!" She flew to her feet, pacing on the carpet in front of him. After a few seconds she kicked a fat historical romance and whirled around at him. "And he doesn't just want to know if you can still write, Jonathan. He wants to know if you've been writing during the past two years. He wants to know not just if you have another book in you, but if you have another book *finished.*"

He looked at her calmly. Why, he wondered, did this wild, beautiful woman make him feel so happy and free? "But you don't know, do you?"

"How much do you want to bet that after he's through with me, *he'll* know?"

"Sweetheart, Wolfe and I spent half of yesterday together. You can't tell him anything about me he couldn't have seen for himself."

"You were on guard with Wolfe," she said. "You weren't with me."

"You're forgetting I knew all along that he sent you."

She stopped dead. "Are you saying that you *have* been on guard with me? Jonathan, I—Have you lied to me?"

"No, I just haven't told you everything."

"Then you don't trust me." She threw up her hands. "Why should you? You'd be in an even worse mess."

"Darling, I trust you. I even trust Wolfe—to a degree. But I've been away for two years. I *have* to do this right, Meg. I have to be ready, and I can't make a mistake. For both our sakes." He rose and took her by the elbows, pulling her stiff, confused body to him. "I

149

want to do what's right, Meg, not just for me, but for you too. For us. Please, trust *me.*"

She sank her head against his chest. "I can't go through with it."

"Darling, Wolfe knows the kind of shape I'm in. He'll interrogate you just to confirm what he already knows. Trust me, you're not going to come between us. I won't let that happen. And I will say this much for Wolfe: I don't think he'll let it happen either."

"You heard him, Jonathan. He wants a full report."

He smiled into her eyes. "So give him one."

"Damn it, Jonathan McGavock, you've turned my whole life upside down—and now I could lose my job *and* you and . . ." She stopped, sniffled, and glared up at him. "How can you stand there and look so calm!"

"Because I am calm."

"Then you *don't* understand."

"I understand that you've turned my life upside down too. Meg, I've been waiting for you to storm into my life for years—forever. I knew when you started talking about story hour at the library and lied about your age that you were the woman for me."

"So how come you tossed me into the reject pile?" she asked, momentarily distracted.

He smiled seductively. "I had other plans for you."

She was unconvinced, as always. "Such as?"

"Finding out what your lovely posterior was doing in my corner of Connecticut. As you'll recall, I had already made the Wolfe connection. I knew I'd fallen head over heels for a little sneak."

"Be glad I didn't spy on you."

"Oh, I wish you had. I was waiting for you."

"And I thought I was being so clever. Wolfe—" She sighed and repeated heavily, "Wolfe. Jonathan, your unscrupulous and unethical former agent wants you back and *writing,* and you can bet your eighty-stitch scar that he won't keep me on at his miserable agency unless I deliver you."

Jonathan tried not to grin. "Personally?"

"With your hands and feet tied and an apple stuffed in your mouth. He won't care!" He started to laugh, and she smacked his chest with her fist. "You're impossible!"

"Meg," he said, catching a lock of her hair between two fingers, "meet Wolfe tomorrow morning. Tell him everything."

"And forget about us?"

"Well, you don't have to mention when you shrieked—"

She scowled at him, but he could see the flash of amusement in her eyes. "You know damned well what I'm talking about," she said.

"You're right," he said, letting his fingers drop to her cheek. Her skin felt so soft. He remembered the feel of her breast and the warm skin of her inner thigh. "Don't forget about us, Meg, not for a second. That's what makes all this worth the effort."

She smiled and kissed the tips of his fingers. "But will it work, Jonathan? Your privacy, your integrity as a writer—"

"You do your job, Meg, and let me worry about Ross Greening."

"You talk as if he's another person!"

Jonathan looked past her and was silent for a moment, thinking about the man he had been two years ago. Was he the same man today? "Maybe he is, Meg," he said quietly. "Tell me, who has turned your life upside down? Jonathan McGavock or Ross Greening?"

"Both—neither. Just you. Jonathan, you're all I want."

He smiled tenderly. "I wish it could be that easy."

"Maybe it can be, if I don't go to Wolfe—"

"You have to, Meg. I want you as you are. I won't have you sacrifice a career that means so much to you. That will tear us apart more than anything. Look around you, damn it! Can't you see who you are? You've worked too hard and sacrificed too much to give up now."

"Wolfe has you in his grasp," she said, desperation creeping into her tone. And Jonathan knew he'd gotten through to her: she understood, even if she had to argue awhile longer. "I'm not sure he'll let you go cleanly this time. If you don't play according to his rules, he could hand his Jonathan McGavock/Ross Greening file to the press and let them have a field day. And if he hasn't already fired me, I'll quit. We'll both lose, Jonathan."

"Don't start second-guessing Wolfe, Meg. I've tried, and it doesn't work. Lots of times during the past six years I was positive he'd tell someone who owned the Ross Greening pseudonym, but he never has. He wouldn't even tell you. Do your job, Meg. Wolfe won't ask any more of you."

She wrapped her arms around his back and hugged him close. He could feel her heart beating against his chest and smell his shampoo in her hair. "Jonathan," she breathed, her voice muffled against his shirt, "I don't want to lose you."

"You won't," he said with all the confidence he could muster. "And even if you should mislay me for a while, you're one hell of a bloodhound. You'll find me, Margaret T." When she looked up at him, startled, he covered her mouth with his and kissed her with a hunger that was deeper and more achingly poignant than any he had ever known. "Or I'll find you."

"Jonathan—"

He pressed her lips together with two fingers. "No more, Meg, please. Darling, we'll find a way for us to be together that won't end up tearing us apart. I know we will." He smiled, trying to lighten his mood, and hers. "I have to be heading out. I have an orchard to tend to, remember?"

She nodded and smiled too. "I guess I won't be showing up for work tomorrow."

"Guess not," he said, starting for the door. He looked across at her. "Wolfe pays more than I do, anyway."

"But he can't wield an ax."

Jonathan laughed. "Not a real one, anyway."

She didn't speak again until he opened the door. It was as if she suddenly realized he was going and might not be back for a long time, and there was so much still to be said. He wondered if she realized how very little he'd told her. She didn't even know why he had gone into seclusion two years ago or why his privacy meant so much to him, but maybe none of that mattered—not anymore.

"Jonathan," she said.

He turned, aching to go to her.

She smiled, and the light in her eyes told him she knew he couldn't. "Your little sneak is falling in love with you."

"And your surly woodsman is already in love with you."

His voice croaked, but he shut the door hard behind him. And Meg respected him and loved him enough not to follow.

At precisely ten o'clock the next morning Meg walked into Wolfe's office without knocking. He was arguing on his high-tech telephone, but he didn't look surprised or perturbed that she hadn't waited for his summons. He motioned for her to sit down, but she was already sitting.

"Call me back when you're ready to talk business," he barked and hung up. "Never try to do business before noon on a Monday, Oakes. Remember that."

"More words of wisdom from Michael Wolfe," she said sardonically.

"Still pissed off, eh? You'll get over it." He drank some coffee from a styrofoam cup. Meg had discovered during her first week in his employ that Wolfe purchased a massive cup of coffee every morning on his way to his office and made it last through the entire day. He drank it hot, lukewarm, cold, and even with a film of scum on the top. "So let's get on with it. What the hell happened in Connecticut?"

Meg made herself comfortable in the leather chair across from his desk. "I hate to tell you this, Mr. Wolfe, but the man who was here Saturday isn't Ross Greening." She crossed her ankles and made a point of looking calm. "He's an impostor—no eighty-stitch scar on his inner thigh."

Wolfe grunted. "How the hell would you know?"

"I'm thorough," she said without a blush.

"Your tongue is turning black, Oakes."

"Better than my heart."

"Still a sarcastic chit, aren't you?"

She smiled coolly. "Keeps me out of a job."

"Oh, so that's it."

Wolfe rested back in his larger and more comfortable leather chair and studied his protégée, who boldly returned his scrutiny. He was dressed casually in a silk shirt and gray wool trousers, but a tie and a sport coat were hanging on his closet doorknob. Meg had always wondered if the hair on his chest was as white as the hair on his head, but she didn't particularly care to find out.

After a few moments he chuckled. "Believed me, didn't you, Oakes?" He was sounding downright smug. "Did I have you shaking in your pink sneakers?"

She almost choked. "He told you?"

"Sure, why not?"

"And here I've been trying to protect him!"

"One of your many mistakes, Oakes. McGavock doesn't need protecting—never has. He needs someone to jerk him up by the short hairs, but I'm not big enough to do it, and neither are you." Wolfe tapped his left temple with his index finger. "That's why we use our wits."

Meg folded her hands in her lap—she was wearing a brown lightweight wool suit—and said firmly, *"We,*

155

Mr. Wolfe? I don't think so. Oh, I know you didn't fire me. You used me as your scapegoat instead."

He waved a hand dismissively. "Business."

"You don't think you fooled Jonathan, do you?"

"Of course not. I was just buying time."

"At my expense—and his."

"Crabby this morning, aren't you? Look, he was buying time too. Now, enough chitchat. You're on the job, Oakes, and I want to know everything. So out with it: What happened up there in the boonies?"

Meg scowled. She didn't want to tell him. She wished she had the nerve to get up and walk out. No, that wasn't it. She *did* have the nerve. After working for Michael Wolfe, even for a little over two months, she could probably find a job at another literary agency. She could even hang out her own shingle and become an independent authors' representative. But that wasn't the point. She liked her job. She liked Wolfe. Jonathan was right: They worked well together. Perhaps in a few years she would start up her own agency, but not now. Now she wanted an apprenticeship, a chance to learn from the very best in the business. She realized she really did want to hold on to her job.

And when he had encouraged her to show up this morning, Jonathan had known it would come to this. He had urged her to tell Wolfe everything. And she believed he meant what he had said, that he wasn't testing her loyalties to him.

So she didn't walk out. She began with the morning she'd rented the apartment above the Rocky Springs Free Town Library and ended with Jonathan's return to his orchards early yesterday afternoon. She left out the personal nature of their relationship but was quite certain Wolfe was able to fill in the blanks. He didn't interrupt—not once.

Now he looked at her sharply. "You mean McGavock's not in New York?"

"I don't think so. He said he had an orchard to tend to."

"Do you have his Connecticut phone number?"

"No, I never thought—"

"Should have been the first thing you did," Wolfe grumbled. "What about his New York number?"

She shook her head.

Wolfe hissed. "Hell."

"I don't understand—"

"This could sink us, Oakes. We just bought McGavock all the time he needed. *Damn!*" He calmed down, but Meg could see the wheels turning in his crafty mind. "All right, Oakes. Grab a cab and get yourself over to his apartment. Now."

"But he's not there."

"Do it!"

Meg was on her feet. "Why?"

"Ross Greening vanished on me once. I'll be damned if I'm going to let him do it again."

"He wouldn't. He . . . he just wouldn't."

Wolfe glared at her. "Why? Because you're in love with him? Don't be naïve, Meg."

It was the first time Wolfe had ever called her by her first name. His tone was still harsh and his words brutal, but she knew he did care.

"I will say this," he added as she started for the door. "If there is a woman alive who can handle McGavock, you're it. *Now go!*"

Ten minutes later she was standing on the tweedy all-weather carpet in the foyer of Jonathan's building. His name had been torn off his mailbox and the intercom buzzer to apartment 6–E. Only two tiny spots of dried glue remained.

Meg sank against the cool glass door.

And even if you should mislay me for a while, you're one hell of a bloodhound. You'll find me. . . . Or I'll find you.

He was gone.

She walked back to Wolfe's office and gave him the bad news.

"My fault," he said. "I knew I should have put a tail on him! Hell, I should have knocked his head in and tied him to my desk."

"Isn't that a little drastic? If he doesn't want to deal with you—"

"You're missing the point, Oakes." Not going on to explain, he pushed her back in the direction of the door. "See if you can pick up his scent in Connecticut. Maybe he made a mistake this time."

She stood her ground. "Mr. Wolfe, obviously he doesn't want to be found."

"Horse manure. And can the Mr., will you? Just Wolfe will do. I don't give a damn what McGavock wants, Oakes. He's caused me enough aggravation already—and himself. *Find him!*"

"It's not worth it!" Meg told him. "Why do you want him back? He's finished with writing—"

"Like hell he is," Wolfe said, deadly serious now. "He's been writing all along, Oakes."

She stared, incredulous. "Did he tell you that?"

"Of course not, but I could smell it."

"No," Meg said, shaking her head. "I never saw a book or a sheet of paper or a typewriter—"

"Sure you did," Wolfe interrupted quietly.

"I did not!"

He sighed. "The guest room, Oakes."

"What?"

Wolfe was growing impatient. "Why the hell do you think he didn't show you his guest room?"

"But that's ridiculous!" She could feel her panic growing, not to mention her confusion. Who was this man she'd fallen in love with? "Jonathan McGavock wouldn't lock himself up in a New York apartment to write."

"No, but Ross Greening would."

And then she understood.

Wolfe took her by the shoulders and shoved her out the door. "Now *go!*"

She went.

The Labrador, Othello, was asleep on the lawn in front of the farmhouse, the Rover and the tractor were parked out back, and the cat was stretched out in the middle of the kitchen table. Art Pesky was there having lunch. He invited Meg in, tossed the cat off the table, and poured her a glass of cider.

"Yep," he said, although she hadn't asked a question, "Jonathan left last night. Packed up a few things and off he went. Does that every now and again."

"Did he say where he was going?"

"Nope."

"What about when he'd be back?"

"Nope." Art scratched the back of his leathery neck. "I didn't ask. Figured it ain't my business."

There was no condemnation of Meg's unbridled curiosity in Art's voice. "Asked me to look out for the place, and I said I would."

"Did he say for how long?"

"Nope."

"Are you supposed to find someone to rent it?"

"Nope."

"Did he say anything else?"

Art hesitated.

"Please."

He shrugged. "Said to beware of women in pink sneakers."

Meg almost collapsed with tension. "Was he smiling when he said it?"

"Like a Cheshire cat."

Mrs. Hennessee at the Rocky Springs post office told Meg that Jonathan had left no forwarding address and she wasn't aware he was even out of town. She obviously wanted to settle down for a good gossip session, but Meg didn't oblige her. "I'm sure it's my mistake," she mumbled and left.

Maybe Art Pesky was supposed to pick up Jonathan's mail—*and forward it?* No, Meg thought; Art had said Jonathan hadn't told him where he was going. Then maybe Jonathan planned to stop by the post office occasionally to pick up his mail. Or maybe he didn't. Maybe he didn't care about his mail. The royalty statements on his three books, which Wolfe had agented, came only twice a year and weren't due for months. Probably everything else was routed through his lawyer, banker, or Art. Or just plain didn't matter to him.

"Maybe, maybe, maybe," she muttered in disgust.

Clouds were gathering. She trudged up to her apartment above the library and turned on all the lights, but it was still a damp and dreary afternoon. She made a cup of tea and dug the lemon meringue pie out of the refrigerator.

You're one hell of a bloodhound. You'll find me.

Ha! She didn't even know where to begin looking!

She sliced off a huge piece of pie. If she were Jonathan McGavock, she thought, where would she go? If she were Ross Greening, where would she go? She groaned and sat down alone at her table with her pie and her cup of tea and her doubts.

She had no answers.

After her tea and pie she walked to Granger's Market in the drizzle. Mr. Granger said hello and asked her how her apple picking was going. She almost burst into tears but managed not to and told him it was going fine. Then she called Wolfe.

"He's gone," she said. "Hasn't even left a crumb for me to follow."

"I figured. I talked to Manuel. Greening's given up his dining room—after three and a half years."

"That's drastic, isn't it?"

"Drastic is Greening's style."

"You don't have to use his pseudonym with me," Meg pointed out dryly.

"Yeah, I guess not. Depressed?"

"Not really. I have a feeling he had this planned for a while."

"His escape route," Wolfe said heavily. "Damn it, when the hell is he going to learn he doesn't have to escape from his own agent?"

"Whatever did you do to him, Wolfe?"

"Sold his books, Oakes. Sold his books."

She had never heard Wolfe sound so low.

"We've lost him, Meg. I'm sorry. You want some time off?"

Meg was tempted. If she stayed in Rocky Springs and continued to work at McGavock Orchards, she might stumble onto a clue . . . or Jonathan himself. But how long could she stay there? The job was only temporary. Apple season wouldn't last forever.

Or I'll find you. . . .

Well, let him! He may have left town grinning like a Cheshire cat, but Meg was getting damned irritated with one handsome and mysterious writer/woodsman.

"No," she said firmly. "I'll be in my office at nine tomorrow morning. And Michael?"

Wolfe grunted.

"Thank you," she said and hung up.

CHAPTER NINE

Two weeks later the mysterious letter arrived. It was addressed directly to her at the Michael Wolfe Literary Agency, and the only return address was Cherryplain, New York. Meg had never heard of Cherryplain, New York. She thought of Jonathan, but that didn't surprise her; she always thought of Jonathan. He was always there, hovering in her thoughts, affecting her moods. She cursed him, she missed him, she loved him . . . and she wanted him back.

But she would be patient. She would work hard and never give up hope.

She sighed and read the letter:

Dear Ms. Oakes:

I saw in *Publishers Weekly* that you're working with the Wolfe agency, and would like to know if you'd be interested in reading three chapters and a story outline of my first mainstream novel. The style is reminiscent of Ross Greening's, but the book is not a thriller. It is, rather, the story of a man coping in a world in which he never expected to find himself—and a woman who straddles both his worlds.

I look forward to hearing from you at your earliest convenience.

Sincerely,

Paul A. Red

P.S. Do you charge a reading fee?

Meg dug out her atlas and pinpointed the town of Cherryplain on Route 22 in the Taconic Valley, about two hours north of Manhattan. She frowned. Who the devil was this Paul Red character? His name sounded vaguely familiar, but that didn't necessarily mean anything.

She showed Wolfe the letter. "So?" he said, unimpressed.

"He mentions Greening," she pointed out.

"Lots of people wish they had Greening's style."

"Any suggestions?"

"Is there an SASE?"

SASE was the vernacular for a stamped, self-addressed return envelope. Meg shook her head.

"Toss it," Wolfe decreed.

Meg returned to her desk and reread the letter. Maybe mentioning Greening had been Mr. Red's mistake. Wolfe hadn't mentioned his renowned former client since that disastrous Monday when Jonathan McGavock, aka Ross Greening, had given him the slip. Meg wasn't sure if he was cutting his losses, assumed she was still on the case, knew something she didn't know, or was sparing her the presumed agony of talking about him.

But talking about Jonathan was never agony, because she knew he'd be back. Or she'd find him—eventually.

She wheeled a sheet of the agency's stationery into her typewriter and polished off a quick note:

Dear Mr. Red:

I would be interested in reading your proposal. Please send it along to me as soon as possible, and remember to enclose a return postage. The agency does not charge a reading fee.

You can expect to hear from me within two weeks of receipt of your manuscript.

Sincerely,

Margaret T. Oakes

Three days later one of the more reliable air express carriers delivered a package from Cherryplain, New York. Inside were three typed chapters, a twenty-page story outline, an SASE, and a tiny cellophane envelope holding a single twenty-cent stamp. And a note:

Dear Ms. Oakes:

Thank you for your interest in my work, and I apologize for not having enclosed an SASE with my letter of inquiry.

I look forward to hearing from you within two weeks.

Sincerely,

Paul A. Red

Meg frowned. The letter was too polite, bordering on the obsequious. She held the flimsy sheet of paper up to the light. Not even one typo. Well, she thought, dumping the letter and the proposal into her canvas bag to take home, at least she'd given it a try. There had been an outside chance that Paul Red was also Jonathan McGavock/Ross Greening.

But he wasn't.

The ache came over her suddenly . . . the sense of loss, of panic, of utter desolation. She needed Jonathan in her life!

She told the receptionist she was going home early to get some reading done, and went.

In the privacy of her apartment she compared Mr. Red's note to those she had received from Jonathan in another lifetime. Even poor Mr. Red's cramped signature didn't compare to Jonathan's arrogant scrawl. And the two styles were completely opposite.

Mr. Paul A. Red of Cherryplain, New York, was dreaming.

She deposited the proposal onto the appropriate stack and stood staring down at the gloomy street, thinking, remembering, letting her despair grow and fester. She couldn't go on. Not anymore, not like this. Leaving work early, giving amateur writers false encouragement, waiting for Jonathan to stroll back into her life—she'd go crazy!

She grabbed her coat, locked up her apartment, and didn't look back.

It was dusk when she parked her Honda in front of the Rocky Springs Free Town Library. The building was closed up and dark, and she realized it was dinnertime in the country. The air was cooler, brisker than in the city, the streets quieter. But even in the dim light Meg could see that the leaves had turned. The giant maple in the library's side lawn was aglow with oranges and yellows. Her mood lifted, and she almost skipped up the stairs. Although she knew he wasn't there, somehow she felt closer to Jonathan.

She fixed herself a TV dinner for supper and read for a while before going to bed. She could see his dark auburn-tinted hair, his taunting gray-green eyes, his broad shoulders. She could hear his laugh, and his promises. It was almost as if he were beside her, and she could actually reach out and run her hands across his hard, lean body.

She hugged her pillow close and fell asleep.

Sometime later, toward dawn, she awoke to a soft tapping on her door. Conditioned by life in New York, she was instantly alert and reaching for a phone she didn't have. She quickly settled on the lamp.

"Meg?"

She leaped out of bed. *"Jonathan!"*

She tore open the door and threw herself into his arms. His deep, sensual laugh, the smell and feel of him, his strength—all combined to intoxicate her and make her dizzy with a hundred different emotions. She sank her head against his warm, woolly sweater. His strong arms enfolded her, and she felt the tears running hot down her cheeks.

"Darling," he said languidly, "don't you think you should have made sure it was me first?"

She shook her head. "I knew it was you," she murmured into his sweater.

"We should get out of the doorway, don't you think?" he suggested wryly.

"Oh, good heavens!" She laughed, suddenly aware that she was wearing exactly nothing. "I—um—didn't bring along a nightgown."

She looked up and saw the flash of his seductive grin against the night. "That's just fine with me."

With one hand, the other still secured around her, he pulled the door shut, then held her close again, stroking the cool skin of her sides and hips. She drank in his touch, his presence, his maleness. Inside her blood boiled hotter than her tears, and then finally the tears stopped and she was looking at him, seeing him as if for the first time, holding back nothing of herself.

"Jonathan . . . oh, God, I've missed you! Where have you been? What—"

"No," he whispered, "not now."

His thumbs skimmed the tips of her breasts, and she inhaled sharply. "You're right," she managed to say, "not now."

"Pretend you're dreaming," he said huskily, moving his mouth down toward hers, even as she could stand waiting no longer and tilted her head up. Their mouths joined, and Meg was still for a moment, just touching, remembering, exulting in the ache that had grown inside her and now had a hope of being fulfilled.

They moved toward the bed, and Meg did feel as if she were in a dream. Everything was perfect. There was no awkwardness, no tentativeness, no doubt. She lay on the bed and watched as he rid himself of his sweater and jeans and everything else that stood between them and their passion, and she could feel her body yearning for him, pinpoint every place that cried out for his touch.

At last he came to her, kissing her lingeringly, tenderly, pressing his hard nakedness against her. She ran her fingers into his hair and knew that he, like she, was ready. The days apart, remembering, longing, dreaming, had been preliminary enough. She moved beneath him, arching slightly, and he came into her, slowly, giving her, and himself, time to savor the moment of their union. Her tongue coursed into his mouth, moving in unison with her hips, and he responded with a deep moan. Beneath her fingertips she could feel the base of his spine tense, and she was prepared for the hard thrust, welcomed it. Another followed, and then she was thrashing beneath him, not thinking but hungering, aching, begging for more of him, giving of herself, responding. Then there was no more to give, but he asked for more. And she gave. He cried out, and she knew instinctively that he had had no more to give either, but gave, and wanted, and soon they were moaning together, moving together, grasping, holding . . . and then still.

She fell asleep encased in him, at peace, totally in love.

When Meg awoke, she was alone in the double bed. Jonathan was gone. Or had he never been there? She looked around, but the only sign of what had passed between them last night was the rumpled bed linens. Had it all been a dream?

If it had, she thought as she trudged to the kitchen, then she had an incredible imagination.

A McGavock Orchards envelope lay on her red

Formica countertop. In place of an address was a penciled note: "Six A.M. I'm up with the crows, love, but you're sound asleep. I've missed you. Two more weeks and this will be over. J."

She turned the envelope over and peered inside, but that was all. No explanation, no promises, no return address. "No nothing!" Meg roared.

Instead of falling into his arms she should have sat him under a hot light and interrogated him!

Wolfe would have.

What had last night *meant?* Where had he come from? How had he known she would be there?

Why had he left?

And what in blazes did he mean by "Two more weeks and this will be over"?

"Two more weeks of this, McGavock, and I'll be a babbling idiot!"

Oh, God, but last night had been so exquisite . . . and not a dream at all. She could remember every detail, every second.

"Blast it all," she moaned.

If only she'd awakened at six! But two weeks on her Manhattan time schedule had reconditioned her to getting up at eight—although there had been those mornings when she had awakened at dawn and imagined Jonathan beside her.

No more, she thought. She was finished. She put up with enough weird writers every day without falling in love with one!

But how was she supposed to *not* fall in love with him? He was so . . . endearing. Masculine. Seductive.

"Infuriating," she muttered.

But he was also an intensely private and solitary man, and she sensed he needed space and time. And she was mature enough—loved him enough—to grant him that space and time. Even if she found it totally mysterious and completely exasperating.

"But what the hell is the man up to?"

Not even venturing a guess, she drank her coffee and drove up to McGavock Orchards. Naturally no one had seen him since that Sunday night when he had packed up and left. Meg bought a half-dozen apple dumplings and a bag of apples and headed back to New York.

She gave Wolfe a dumpling, but she didn't tell him she had seen Ross Greening.

Exactly two weeks later, when Meg was at her wits' end, alternately convinced she would never see Jonathan again and that he was going to walk through the door the next second, another letter from Paul Red of Cherryplain, New York, appeared on her desk. She groaned when she saw the name, and remembered the proposal, still occupying space on her apartment floor, unread. She didn't think Mr. Red would understand that she was hopelessly behind in her reading because of a certain apple grower/forester/thriller writer who was driving her nuts.

Knowing exactly the kind of overly polite and apologetic letter she would get, Meg wearily opened the letter. The polite pests, she thought, were always the worst. She looked forward to bursting the bubbles of bona fide jerks, but the Paul A. Reds of the world required more finesse. And made her feel a whole lot more guilty.

She was in the mood for receiving a little tender loving care, not dishing it out. With a heavy sigh she read:

Dear Ms. Oakes:

Your two weeks are up. What did you think of my proposal?

Sincerely,

Paul A. Red

P.S. What do agents do with SASE's that never get returned?

Meg threw back her head and laughed. *Good for you, Mr. Paul A. Red!* she thought. She'd given him a deadline and with what must have seemed a cavalier disregard for his sensibilities hadn't met it. And he'd called her onto the mat for it.

Then, very abruptly, she stopped laughing and took another look at the letter. There was more than a hint of arrogance in his words. And his signature seemed to her less careful, less cramped. It was much more a scrawl. There were two hastily corrected typographical errors. And his typewriter ribbon needed changing.

Meg canceled a luncheon appointment with one of her favorite editors, told the receptionist she was going home for the day, and hopped on the subway. Twenty minutes later she was plucking Paul Red's proposal out of the appropriate stack. She didn't even bother making a pot of coffee but just plopped down in the middle of her worn Persian carpet and began to read.

It was magnificent.

The style had the strength and vigor of Ross Greening, but the story, even in the three sample chapters, had a depth of feeling, a subtlety of mood, absent—and unnecessary—in Greening's thrillers. And yet it moved. It was a page-turner. A throat-tightener.

A damned good book.

She hailed a cab in front of her building and went back to the office. Wolfe was going over contracts and had decreed he wasn't to be disturbed, but Meg knocked once on his door and walked in. She thrust the proposal at him and said, "Read this."

He gave her a brief, appraising glance and twisted his mouth from one side to another.

"I've been under a lot of stress," she admitted, "but I'm not nuts—yet. Read."

He read two pages before he leaped up, kissed her on both cheeks, and yelled, "Sonofabitch! Didn't I tell you the bastard was still writing?"

Meg's heart was pounding. "Look here, Wolfe, this is by a man named Red. Paul Red."

"Like hell. It's by a man named Greening—your goddamned Jonathan McGavock. Ha-ha! It'll be a blockbuster!"

Red . . . Greening . . . Meg asked hoarsely, "You're sure?"

It was a stupid question: Wolfe was always sure.

He insisted on keeping the proposal. He even had his secretary make extra copies. Meg returned to her apartment and tracked down an apple cookbook she had purchased at McGavock Orchards. And there, in the section on apples, was what she had hoped and dreaded she'd find.

Paula Reds were a variety of apple.

173

CHAPTER TEN

Meg drove straight up Route 22 to Cherryplain. It was picturesque, just a cluster of houses off the highway in the narrow but beautiful Taconic Valley. If worse came to worst, she figured she could drive around and see who had a black Porsche parked in their driveway. It wouldn't take that long. First, however, she tried the post office, which, she was surprised to discover, was even smaller than the one in Rocky Springs.

But Paul A. Red didn't live in Cherryplain. "I've never met the man myself," explained the postal worker, a cheerful woman around Meg's age, "but we get mail for him every now and then. We just forward it. He's a friend of a forester who owns land up in one of the hollows."

Meg nearly choked. "Jonathan McGavock?"

"Right. Course, he doesn't live here either—just shows up once in a while to check on his trees."

Jonathan had mentioned that he owned a considerable amount of land. Why had Meg assumed it was all in or near Rocky Springs? She was disgusted with herself for not even *thinking* of checking into Jonathan's holdings. She might have tracked him down weeks ago!

"Yes, I know Jonathan," she said smoothly. "Do you have Mr. Red's forwarding address?"

"Sure." She turned her back for a moment; then neatly printed a few lines on a note pad, tore off the sheet, and handed it to Meg. "There you go."

Meg said thank you but didn't look at the address until she was outside. Then she thought the sun had blinded her. It couldn't be! But it was. Paul A. Red's mail was forwarded to the care of Jonathan McGavock, not in Rocky Springs, Connecticut, but in New York, New York.

On *Park Avenue* in New York, New York.

Irritated that she'd wasted so much time, Meg glanced at her watch. She could be back in New York before dinner.

She parked her car in her garage and took a cab over to Park Avenue. The building was very impressive indeed. Meg was greeted by a spit-and-polish doorman who didn't believe for an instant that she had legitimate business with Jonathan McGavock. Before she let loose with an indignant protest, she caught sight of her reflection in a giant mirror in the lobby. Her hair was windblown, her face was somewhat pallid, and her beige linen pants were ingloriously wrinkled. That was one thing about linen, she thought. She looked as though she needed a good night's sleep, a long hot bath, and a change of clothes. She felt it too.

So she changed her tactics. Instead of coming on as a pushy local, she approached the doorman and explained that she had just arrived in New York and had driven there *herself,* and she was anxious to make connections with Mr. McGavock so she could get some rest. The doorman was instantly sympathetic. She drove in from the country? She must have been on the road for days! And she drove alone—in a car? To New York? The poor woman! She must be exhausted! No wonder she looked like a wreck! Ah, but to have arrived in civilization at last.

"I will call Mr. McGavock at once. Your name again, miss?"

"Oakes," she said. "Margaret T. Oakes."

A moment later he told her Mr. McGavock said to go right up and guided her to the elevator, personally showing her how it worked. "It goes slow, miss," he assured her. "No need to worry."

She thanked him and as the elevator made its way up to the eighth floor debated slapping on some lipstick or something so she wouldn't look quite so disheveled. Why should she? Let Jonathan McGavock/Ross Greening/Paul A. Red see just exactly what his shenanigans had done to her!

The elevator opened into a plush foyer. Meg had already figured it would be a floor-through condominium, but this confirmed her suspicion. She tapped on a locked silver-trimmed door.

Jonathan opened the door, and Meg had to steel herself to keep from swinging into his arms. He looked urbane and masculine in a cashmere sweater and double pleat linen trousers. His didn't have wrinkles. His hair was thick and dark and shining. She thought of her fingers running through it, and his fingers running through hers.

The shock of seeing him in an elegant New York condominium threw off her timing and gave him the

176

chance to get in the first word. "Took you long enough, love," he said in his delectable lazy baritone.

She recovered and pretended not to hear him. "Mr. Red?" she said, annoyed that she sounded hoarse. "My, but it's been an adventure tracking you down. My name is Margaret Oakes. I'm with the Wolfe agency here in New York. You sent me your proposal, remember?"

His brow furrowed, and she couldn't tell if he was concerned or irritated. Or both. "Meg." There was a distinct warning in his tone.

Ignoring it, she pushed past him into the living room, which was obviously in the midst of being decorated. Either that or Jonathan had given up furniture. "Michael Wolfe and I have read your proposal," she went on briskly, "and I wanted to talk to you personally about it. I didn't expect to find you here in New York, of course. I tried Cherryplain first, naturally, but—well, you are elusive, Mr. Red. But I'm glad I've found you."

Jonathan had shut the door and was now standing with his hands on his lean hips, watching her—but not indulgently. His eyes weren't twinkling.

She cocked her head sideways. "You *are* Paul Red, aren't you?"

"Meg," he said darkly, "I'm going to give you five seconds. If you haven't cut this Paul Red line, I'm going to—I don't know what I'll do, but it won't be pleasant."

"My, my." She gave an exaggerated shrug. "Then you're not Paul Red. Where do you suppose I can find him?"

"Meg!"

"Of course, we'll have to find an appropriate pseudonym for him. Paul Red just isn't dramatic enough." She waved a hand Wolfe style. "But that's not your concern. Why, sir, you look upset and—What are you doing?" She started backing up, but he kept moving toward her. "Now, look here, mister, I . . . *Jonathan!*"

He caught her around the middle and dropped her neatly onto the thick carpeted floor, breaking her fall with his arm. She started to laugh. "You asked for it, Oakes," he growled and began tickling her unmercifully.

And then the tickles turned to caresses, and his mouth was on hers, and they began pulling off their clothes, laughing, teasing, until they were naked and making love in the empty room.

"That, Mr. McGavock/Greening/Red," Meg said later, slipping on her shirt, "was not very urbane of you."

He leaned back on his elbows, not deigning to slip into anything at all. "More on the surly side?"

"The woodsman in you, I'm sure."

"Mustn't stereotype people, Ms. Oakes."

She scoffed. "If the shoe fits . . ."

"I didn't hear you complaining," he pointed out.

"Me complain? No, never. My apple grower turns into a famous writer, they both sweep me off my feet, and then they disappear and I hear from this borderline nurd who—"

Jonathan laughed. "Poor Paul. Wait until I tell him what you said."

"Spare me, McGavock," she said with mock severity. "As I was saying, I hear from dear Mr. Red, who sends me an absolutely amazing proposal for a book, only when I go to find him, it turns out he's living in New York City and is actually my apple grower and famous writer. So instead of falling in love with just two men, I'm now having to fall in love with three men—all of whom just combined forces and attacked me on the rug in . . . *What is this place?*"

"My condominium," he said wryly.

"Oh."

"I couldn't quite come up with a penthouse," he said irreverently and changed the subject. "I suppose you want to know what this last month has been about?"

She sighed, loving him now as much as ever, feeling as if she would burst just with the pressure of all her emotions . . . and all her questions. "I want to know what the last two years have been about. Jonathan, who are you?"

He rolled onto his side, grabbed her hand, and pulled her to him, kissing her. "You know better than anyone, Meg," he whispered.

"I don't mean that."

"I know." With a grace Meg now took for granted, he leaned on one elbow, lying on his side. Satiated as she was, she longed to touch him again . . . and again and again. "It's not a long story, darling, or a very complicated one, really. Has Wolfe told you anything?"

"Not a word."

"He's a closemouthed bastard, isn't he? Possibly his only endearing trait."

She laughed. "True."

"All right, I'll begin at the beginning. I'm a forester,

Meg. I did my undergraduate work at Michigan and my graduate work at Berkeley. I did some work for the Forest Service during school, and afterward they took me on in forest management. I lived and worked in some pretty isolated places, but I enjoyed it. I'd be happy, Meg, if I'd never put pen to paper. I mean that."

She smiled and said quietly, "I know."

"But I did begin to write—while I was with the service. I was just having a good time with it, but from the very beginning I decided my writing—whatever became of it—wasn't going to interfere with my life. So I created Ross Greening. I was enjoying my solitary life, and I figured I didn't want to ruin it just because I'd sold a couple of books." He sighed. "I never figured on selling *millions* of books."

"Must have made living a solitary life a chore," Meg put in.

"It was interesting, to say the least. Keeping the two identities just sort of happened—and it was fun for a while. But it became more and more difficult to keep Ross Greening from infringing on my life as Jonathan McGavock, and vice versa. Pretty soon I had two distinct sets of friends, one for each identity. Wolfe was all for integrating the two and giving up all the secrecy, but I was reluctant to let the man I'd been die. I knew it had to happen, but I wanted it to happen my way—not Wolfe's."

"Wolfe would want you to milk it for all the publicity you could get," Meg said pragmatically. "And you wouldn't. Was that when you decided to disappear?"

He shook his head. "Not quite. While all this mess was going on I was also working on another book. I told Wolfe it wasn't going to be a thriller, and he hit the ceiling. He went into his whole bit about marketing strategy and all that, but I'm a writer, Meg, and I had a book in me that needed to get out." He shrugged and said offhandedly, "So I said to hell with Wolfe and to hell with Ross Greening, and I took off. I bought the place in Rocky Springs, gave Wolfe my post office box number so he could send me my royalty statements, and told him I didn't want to see his face on pain of death."

"Were you that dramatic?"

"It took Wolfe two years to get up the courage even to send someone else after me, didn't it?"

Meg tried not to laugh. "He probably thought you'd come after him with a chain saw or an ax or something."

Jonathan grunted. "I might have, the bastard."

"He was just looking after your best interests," she pointed out reasonably. "He always says all his clients have the right to disagree with him; they just don't usually have the stomach for it."

"You just made that up."

"I did not."

"He never told me that." Jonathan grinned and winked at her. "It'll be good having a spy in his office."

"I'm his associate," she averred.

"You see the human side to everyone, don't you Margaret T.?"

"Even surly woodsmen," she said, smiling. "You've got two more years to go, McGavock."

"All right. For the next two years I wrote and played forester and apple grower. It was peaceful, but

I missed being Ross Greening. I wasn't sure exactly what I was going to do about it—or when. And then along came a beautiful and decidedly outspoken woman who showed me how exciting and easy it would be to integrate Ross Greening into my life—not to mention her, of course. So I figured, what the hell?" He sat up and reached for his pants. "The rest was just a question of timing and logistics."

She sat for a moment, waiting for him to go on, but he just calmly got dressed.

"That's it?" she said.

"What else do you want to know?"

"Lots!"

"Beginning with?"

"Your book. You said you wrote for two years. Were you working on the book you just sent me?"

"Yep."

"Don't pull an Art Pesky on me, Jonathan. Is that the book Wolfe didn't want you to write?"

He grinned. "Yes, Margaret, that's the book Wolfe didn't want me to write, but which I wrote anyway."

"He loves it, you know. I mean, he only read two pages—"

"That's all he ever reads."

"Says it'll be a blockbuster."

"Especially if I use the Ross Greening name, hmm?"

"Well, yes, I suppose."

"I don't intend to."

Meg hesitated. "He'll advise you to use it."

"You?"

"I'm not your agent."

"That's not what I asked."

"You won't tell Wolfe?"

He grinned. "Surly woodsman's honor."

"I'd say it's up to you."

"Do I detect a *but?*"

"But if I *were* your agent, I would point out that you've established a large readership with the Ross Greening name and your book would be worth more to a publisher, and therefore to you, if you used his name."

"You're talking dollars and cents, right?"

She nodded. "Agents usually do."

"I'm not."

"I know," she said quietly.

He went down on one elbow and kissed her hard on the mouth. "There you go, you're hired."

"As what?"

"My agent. Screw Wolfe."

"Jonathan!"

"All right, all right. We'll work something out. Maybe Wolfe can be Ross Greening's agent."

Groaning in total exasperation, she pounced on him, wrapping her legs around his waist and leaping onto his back piggyback style. He didn't budge. "You're driving me nuts!" she exclaimed.

"Is it my massive shoulders, love, or just my overpowering sensuality?"

"It's your warped sense of humor!"

He plucked her off his back and sat her down beside him. "Better a warped sense of humor than—"

"Whatever you're going to say, don't. I want to know how Wolfe can be Ross Greening's agent if you want to write as Jonathan McGavock."

"Elementary, my dear Oakes. I want to write as

183

Ross Greening as well. I rather like the fellow, although he does have this penchant for disappearing for days at a time to write in furnished New York apartments."

"You mean—"

"I mean I have a Ross Greening novel completed." His eyes gleamed merrily. "Wolfe will love the first two pages."

"Jonathan, that's wonderful! Two books! I can't wait to tell Wolfe! He insisted you were writing. I don't know how he does it."

"I don't either," Jonathan admitted grudgingly.

"What about the apartment we went to—the one with the exposed brick walls?"

"One of my many retreats. Wolfe didn't tell you that much?"

"No, the—" She stopped herself and looked menacing instead.

"The what, love?"

"Never mind. One doesn't curse one's colleagues in front of a client."

"Want me to fire you, then?"

"No! Good heavens, I'd be in for it then, wouldn't I? To have you slip out of Wolfe's clutches *three* times —He wouldn't be happy just firing me. Now go on. Wolfe knew you liked to hole up in New York to write?"

"He's the one who got me started. It was after the chain saw accident. I was supposed to be working on a book, but I wasn't getting much accomplished. I used to do my best writing in the woods, but that was before it became a retreat from being a writer. Wolfe pointed out that going out and contemplating 'the goddamn wilderness' didn't get books written, and if what I needed was solitary confinement, there was no place like New York. I tend to write thrillers in a frenzy of sorts. They don't take that long, but it's an intense experience. This other book was different. Does this make any sense to you, Meg?"

"No, but I'm not one of your creative types," she said, tongue in cheek.

"Would you like a thrashing?"

"Sounds exciting."

"Woman, you have a devious imagination—for an uncreative type. Now—"

"I'm not through with you," she warned.

His eyes twinkled. "No?"

He rubbed her thigh, and suddenly she felt suffused with warmth. Had she ever been this happy? "What about Paul Red?" she asked, sounding more breathless and dreamy than intimidating.

"I needed a little more time to put all the pieces into place. I'd compromised you enough with Wolfe, and I had to get away for a while to get my manuscripts into submittable form and figure a way out of this mess. Sometimes I have to be alone, Meg. That's just the way I am."

"I think I'm mature enough to accept that," she said quietly, "and in love with you enough."

He smiled, his eyes searching her face, obviously liking what he saw. "That's what I was counting on," he said. "Paul A. Red was just my warped sense of humor and flare for drama. He was your clue, Margaret T. I thought you'd see through him right away."

"I'm not *that* up on my apple varieties—and your Mr. Red was a little tentative."

"I didn't want to make it *too* easy." He scooped her up into his arms and rolled onto his back, with her on his stomach, laughing down into his eyes. "Happy, darling?"

"More than happy, Jonathan; lots more."

"I love you, Margaret T. I thought of you every day and every night while I was gone. Sometimes I wondered if I'd ever want to go off alone again—and it was a nice feeling, my darling, to know that you were waiting for me. That probably sounds as presumptuous as hell—"

"No," she interrupted, "no, it doesn't. It sounds wonderful. I was confused while you were gone, Jonathan, and angry sometimes, and afraid, but it was good for me too. It helped me put my life into perspective. And us. Jonathan, I'm in love with you—whoever and whatever you want to be. But I kept wondering if you'd come back and ask me to move to Montana with you. I kept wondering if you'd ask me to change so that we could be together."

"Darling Meg, I love you as you are."

"A messy New York literary agent who doesn't read proposals within two weeks?"

"As the outspoken and courageous woman who can put up with a surly, cantankerous woodsman—as anything you choose to be, so long as you choose it."

"And so long as I don't tell you who to be?"

"Darling, I want us to be together and grow together, but we're not two halves of the same nut. We're two—" He laughed, gathering her up into his arms. "We're two perfectly whole nuts on our own!"

They laughed for a long time, hugging each other, murmuring words of love, promises, hopes. After a while Jonathan put on his shirt and gave her a bare-foot tour of the condominium.

"Three bedrooms, study, living room, office, dining room, kitchen, laundry room complete with a service elevator," he explained. "Your average New York floor-through. I tried for a penthouse, love, but you must know what the real estate situation is like in New York."

"Don't I ever," she agreed, taking his hand. "The rent I pay on my apartment could feed a small African country."

"We have great views of Park Avenue, though."

"We?" she said dubiously. "You, Ross, and Paul?"

He smiled. "No, you and I. Rocky Springs will be our second home, but I figured it was time to settle into a permanent place here in the city. And with all your junk and mine, I decided we'd need space."

"Jonathan, what are you saying?"

His smile took on a glimmer of mischief. "I did say junk, didn't I? Just an expression, love. Your employer or partner or whatever he is may get under my skin once in a while, but I know you're only *slightly* un-scrupulous and unethical. If you can live with surly and cantankerous, I can live with unscrupulous and—"

"McGavock!"

"Yes, m'love?"

She grinned up at him, the light in her eyes reflected in his. "Are you suggesting I move in with you?"

"Oh, yes," he said huskily, taking her into his arms. "Oh, yes, indeed." His mouth moved slowly toward hers. "Will you marry me, Margaret T.?"

"Oh, yes," she said, "oh, yes, indeed."

The next morning they went together to tell Wolfe. "Married?" He grunted. "Good. That's one way to keep track of you, McGavock. Here, sit down. I've got some ideas on what to do with your next Greening book."

Jonathan eyed Meg dangerously, but she shook her head innocently, denying that she'd told Wolfe a thing. She hadn't had a chance! She and Jonathan had been together every second since she'd found him yesterday afternoon.

"How do you know I have a Greening book?" Jonathan demanded.

"I've known you too long, McGavock. Now sit down and tell me about it. Oakes, where the hell are you going? Sit. Now. Both of you. First things first. This Red character has to go. You know that, right?"

Jonathan felt the familiar gnawing in his stomach of pure aggravation that he experienced whenever he dealt with his agent. "Look, here, Wolfe—"

"The name won't sell. Doesn't go with the book. Too wimpy, you know? Paul A. Red. I suggest publishing it under your own name. I know, I know. You like to go off into the wilderness and commune with nature or whatever the hell it is you do." Wolfe pronounced *wilderness* with scathing contempt. "But I ask you, do the goddamn squirrels and bears know Ross Greening from a canary? And those meatheads you hang out with—what the hell do they care? So—"

"Wolfe," Jonathan interrupted patiently, "Meg and I have been over this."

Wolfe shot his associate a look. "Oakes?"

"He's willing to do this new book as Jonathan McGavock and admit he's also Ross Greening."

"You can't kill off Greening!"

"I don't intend to," Jonathan said, almost lazily.

Understanding dawned, and Wolfe leaped up. Jonathan expected some kind of outburst, but Wolfe walked around the desk, stuck out his hand, and said, "Welcome back, Jonathan." Then he turned to Meg and grinned. "Meg? Good work." He waved both hands as he returned to his desk. "I've got a mountain of work to do. Editors hounding me, lunatic writers calling up. Why don't you two take off for the rest of the week? Oakes, you've been working your ass off. You aren't any good to me half-dead. The three of us will sit down next week and talk. Oh, and McGavock? I'll start leaking word you're Ross Greening while you're out of town. It'll hold down on the publicity."

"Thanks, Wolfe."

"Ah, forget it. Love makes me feel human. Now, will you two take off?"

The first person to find out Jonathan McGavock was also known as Ross Greening was Art Pesky, manager of McGavock Orchards. "You write them spy stories?" he said. "My wife reads those. Don't recall the name Greening, though. I'll have to ask her. Let's see. We've got the lower orchard picked, and . . ."

Jonathan was still laughing about the incident that night when he and Meg were lying together in front of a roaring fire in the big farmhouse living room. Othello was stretched out beside him, and the cat, who had no name, was curled up in Meg's lap. "I almost said, 'But, Art, I'm famous, damn it!' " Jonathan said, still chuckling. "Sweetheart, what am I going to do if all my friends decide to treat me like the same old Jonathan?"

She laughed, laying her head in his lap. "Be glad you have good taste in friends."

"Always count on Margaret T. for an answer."

"Was Art surprised about us?"

"Not in the least. He said he always knew I'd fall for someone in pink sneakers."

"Oh, go on, he said no such thing."

"He did."

"I don't believe you."

Jonathan laughed. "I'm not the consummate liar, remember?"

"Othello! *Attack!*"

Othello paid no attention whatsoever. Jonathan, however, did. "Attack, you say?" he murmured and swung one arm around her. "Glad to oblige, m'love."

Meg laughed. "Jonathan McGavock," she said, trying vainly to give him a good wrestling match, "I want to grow with you, fight with you, and be with you forever. I love you so much I could burst!"

"Don't burst," he murmured and added seductively, "at least not yet."

"For you I won't."

And she didn't, for a while at least.

Now you can reserve March's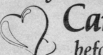
Candlelights
<u>before</u> they're published!

♥ You'll have copies set aside for *you*
   the instant they come off press.
♥ You'll save yourself precious shopping
   time by arranging for *home delivery.*
♥ You'll feel proud and efficient about
   organizing a system that *guarantees* delivery.
♥ You'll avoid the disappointment of not
   finding *every* title you want and need.

ECSTASY SUPREMES $2.50 *each*

☐ 65 **TENDER REFUGE**, Lee Magner 18648-X-35
☐ 66 **LOVESTRUCK**, Paula Hamilton 15031-0-10
☐ 67 **QUEEN OF HEARTS**, Heather Graham 17165-2-30
☐ 68 **A QUESTION OF HONOR**, Alison Tyler 17189-X-32

ECSTASY ROMANCES $1.95 *each*

☐ 314 **STAR-CROSSED**, Sara Jennings 18299-9-11
☐ 315 **TWICE THE LOVING**, Megan Lane 19148-3-20
☐ 316 **MISTAKEN IMAGE**, Alexis Hill Jordan 15698-X-14
☐ 317 **A NOVEL AFFAIR**, Barbara Andrews 16079-0-37
☐ 318 **A MATTER OF STYLE**, Alison Tyler 15305-0-19
☐ 319 **MAGIC TOUCH**, Linda Vail 15173-2-18
☐ 320 **FOREVER AFTER**, Lori Copeland 12681-9-28
☐ 321 **GENTLE PROTECTOR**, Linda Randall Wisdom . 12831-5-19

At your local bookstore or use this handy coupon for ordering:

DELL READERS SERVICE –Dept. B546A
P.O. BOX 1000, PINE BROOK, N.J. 07058

Please send me the above title(s). I am enclosing $_____ (please add 75¢ per copy to cover postage and handling). Send check or money order—no cash or CODs. Please allow 3-4 weeks for shipment.
CANADIAN ORDERS: please submit in U.S. dollars

Ms Mrs Mr _____

Address_____

City State_____ Zip _____

Fans of JAYNE CASTLE rejoice— this is her biggest and best romance yet!

From California's glittering gold coast, to the rustic islands of Puget Sound, Jayne Castle's longest, most ambitious novel to date sweeps readers into the corporate world of multimillion dollar real estate schemes—and the very *private* world of executive lovers. Mixing business with pleasure, they make passion *their* bottom line.

384 pages $3.95

Don't forget Candlelight Ecstasies, for Jayne Castle's *other* romances!